**Matteo stayed behind her, following her from room to room. 'Phoebe... Ms Gates...does this mean you'll take the job?'**

She couldn't speak. Room after room... There were so many thoughts clamouring in her brain about how gorgeous she could make this place that she couldn't form words. Her dream job... The job that could change her whole career... A chance to pay off her mother's medical bills. A chance to move forward. A chance to pull herself out of the fog that had hung around her for the last few years.

'Phoebe.'

His voice grew sharp and he gave her arm a pull, tugging her around to face him. She rested her hands on his upper arms. She couldn't help herself. She almost wanted to give him a kiss on the cheek.

She let out a laugh. 'Will I take the job? Absolutely. Now I've seen it, this place is mine. Matteo, I'm going to do such a good job you're never going to want to let me go.'

It was for the briefest of seconds but a wash of sadness seemed to sweep his face. A whole host of something she really didn't understand. But almost as soon as it had appeared the shutters came down over his eyes again. Matteo Bianchi had the perfect mask. The perfect face for business.

The edges of his lips curved upwards. For the first time since she'd met him the tension in his shoulders actually looked as if it had disappeared a little.

'Phoebe, a quarter of a million dollars for four weeks' work and I *will* let you go.'

Dear Reader,

When I was asked by my editor to write a New Year bride story I was delighted. As romance stories are full of billionaires I was happy to oblige and pick some spectacular settings—a gorgeous house in the Hamptons and a private evening dinner at the Colosseum in Rome. My hero is a billionaire, so why not?

But Matteo is hiding family secrets. His mother killed herself years ago, and although his siblings know what she did they've never been told why. Thirty years ago post-partum psychosis wasn't particularly well known or understood. Thankfully, nowadays things are different, and Matteo's fears for his sister's pregnancy are unfounded.

Enter my lovely sunny heroine, New Yorker Phoebe, an aspiring interior designer who has just been given the job of a lifetime: to dress his house in the Hamptons ready for sale. But Phoebe falls in love with the place—*and* the man who is determined to sell it. Cue an excuse for a scene that might be a little similar to one in *Beauty and the Beast*—see what you think!

Here's hoping that you love this hero and heroine as much as I do. Feel free to contact me via my website: scarlet-wilson.com.

Love,

*Scarlet*

W.G.   MR      I

# THE ITALIAN BILLIONAIRE'S NEW YEAR BRIDE

BY
SCARLET WILSON

First Published in Great Britain 2017
By Mills & Boon, an imprint of HarperCollins*Publishers*
1 London Bridge Street, London SE1 9GF

© 2017 Scarlet Wilson

ISBN: 978-0-263-07520-5

MIX
Paper from
responsible sources
FSC
www.fsc.org
FSC™ C007454

This book is produced from independently certified FSC™ paper
to ensure responsible forest management. For more information
visit www.harpercollins.co.uk/green.

Printed and bound in Great Britain
by CPI Group (UK) Ltd, Croydon, CR0 4YY

**Scarlet Wilson** writes for both Mills & Boon Romance and Medical Romance. She lives on the west coast of Scotland with her fiancé and their two sons. She loves to hear from readers and can be reached via her website: scarlet-wilson.com.

## Books by Scarlet Wilson

### Mills & Boon Romance

#### *Summer at Villa Rosa*
*The Mysterious Italian Houseguest*

#### *Maids Under the Mistletoe*
*Christmas in the Boss's Castle*

#### *Tycoons in a Million*

*Holiday with the Millionaire*
*A Baby to Save Their Marriage*

#### *The Vineyards of Calanetti*
*His Lost-and-Found Bride*

### Mills & Boon Medical Romance

*One Kiss in Tokyo...*
*A Royal Baby for Christmas*
*The Doctor and the Princess*
*A Family Made at Christmas*

Visit the Author Profile page
at millsandboon.co.uk for more titles.

This book is dedicated to my mum and dad,
John and Joanne Wilson, for their continued support
of all my writing endeavours and all the help
they give me with my boys, Elliott and Rhys.

**Praise for
Scarlet Wilson**

# CHAPTER ONE

THE SHRILL RING of the phone invaded her dream just as she was about to save the world with Hugh Jackman. Phoebe stuck her hand out from under the snuggly white duvet and blindly felt around the bedside table as her brain tried to orientate her to time and day. She'd just been about to remove Hugh's shirt...all in the name of saving the world, of course.

After a few fumbles, she finally found the phone and pulled it under the duvet next to her ear. "Phoebe Gates." She winced. The phone was cold, much like the air outside her duvet. New York had spent the last few days covered in a snowstorm and her boiler was behaving like a temperamental teenager.

"Ms. Gates, how would you like to earn a quarter of a million dollars?"

The voice was smooth. Italian. Rich and deep with a timbre she didn't recognize. It was like being smothered in melted chocolate.

"Wh...what?" She snuggled further down under the duvet. Maybe she was still sleeping. Maybe this was all just part of the dream.

"I said how would you like to earn a quarter of a million dollars?"

Phoebe frowned and rolled onto her back. "That would be wonderful."

"Are you free?"

"Excuse me?"

"Are you free for the next month?"

Her brain started to shift gear. "Hey, wait a minute. You're one of those creepy callers, aren't you? Well, you picked the wrong girl. There's no way—"

"Ms. Gates," the voice interrupted her with a hint of impatience but Phoebe had finally started to wake up.

"Well, if you're not a creepy caller you're one of those scam artists. Don't tell me—you just need the details of my checking account and you'll get the money right to me."

She pushed herself up in the bed, wincing at the bright white light everywhere. Snow just seemed to reflect snow. "Do you know what day it is?" She turned to her clock, "And what *time* it is?" She ran her fingers through her thick tangled curls. Thank goodness there was no mirror around. She was definitely the "before" of some kind of wonder conditioner commercial. "It's Boxing Day. It's eight a.m. Haven't you heard of the word *Christmas*?"

There was a loud impatient sigh at the other end of the phone. "Ms. Gates, are you available in the next few weeks or not?"

She was definitely waking up now. Arrogant. He'd invaded the best dream in the world, ruined her lazy morning and he thought he could be snarky?

"That depends entirely who I'm talking to and what you're talking about. You haven't seemed to introduce yourself. In my world, we call those bad manners."

Silence at the end of the phone. Good. Maybe Hugh Jackman was still waiting for her.

"Apologies, Ms. Gates. You're right. My grandmother is currently spinning in her grave and slapping the back of my head."

This time there was almost an edge of humor in his voice.

"Matteo Bianchi. I have a house—two houses in fact—that I need some work done on. I need them dressed and ready to sell in a few weeks."

Work. This really was work. But she couldn't help herself. "And you had to phone me at eight a.m. on Boxing Day morning?"

"Christmas Day is over. I don't like to waste time. Are you available, or not?"

He was getting snarky again. Phoebe shifted position in her bed and looked out at the falling snow. She'd planned on going to the sales. But braving the snow, as well as the chaos of the crowded shops, was slipping further down her list of priorities.

"Where are the houses?" she asked.

"The first is in the Hamptons," he said quickly. "Southampton, to be exact."

She felt her heart rate quicken. The Hamptons. Million-dollar houses with million-dollar budgets. The two things she'd always dreamed of. Particularly as her mother's medical costs mounted.

She tried to stop her voice squeaking. "And the second?" How much had he offered to pay?

"Rome." Her heart plummeted. Rome. An airplane ride away. Probably more than one airplane. Her skin prickled instantly and it wasn't the cold.

"Oh." It was the best response she could do.

"I'd need you to start straight away. I'll make sure you have a company credit card to pay for any work or items that you need."

She hadn't found her voice yet. Her heart was clamouring against her chest wall. Rome. How could she go to Rome?

"Ms. Gates? Are you still there?"

"Yes. The Hamptons is fine. I can look at the house whenever suits. As for the house in Rome—that might be more of an issue."

"Why do you need to see the house?" It didn't matter she hadn't met Mr. Bianchi yet, she could almost picture him frowning.

"I always look over any house before I agree to dress it for sale." He didn't mention the Rome comment.

There was another sigh.

Her curiosity was sparked. She'd never heard of Matteo Bianchi and, with an accent like that, if she'd met him before, she could guarantee she'd remember.

"Fine. I'll pick you up in an hour."

"What?" She sat bolt upright in the bed.

"You want to see the house? I'll pick you up in an hour and you can see the house."

She was stunned. One minute she was in the middle of a blissful dream—next she was working on Boxing Day.

Something pricked in her brain. "Mr. Bianchi, where did you hear about me?"

"I saw the apartment you dressed near Central Park." He paused for a second as her brain caught up. "I liked it."

She couldn't help but smile. "In Madison Court?" She'd loved that job. The apartment belonged to an old sea captain. Other interior designers had suggested ripping the apartment bare, painting all the walls white and tiling all the floors. She'd been the only designer to suggest embracing the whole essence of Captain

Monaghan's life. She'd scaled back some of the clutter and enhanced the whole seafaring lifestyle by focusing on a few key pieces. A ship's wheel. A handcrafted lighthouse. A small-scale model of one of the ships he'd captained. The apartment had sold for well over the asking price—with a key request to keep the design aspects.

A warm feeling spread through her belly. The fact that Matteo had seen her work and liked it made her smile. Madison Court had been her biggest job yet. She hadn't told anyone she'd met the old sea captain when he was getting chemotherapy in the same hospital as her mother. It was funny where some of the turning points in your life could be.

She rested back against the pillows.

"Yes," came the rich smooth voice. "Madison Court was...unusual. So, are you available for the next few weeks?"

A quarter of a million dollars. That was what he'd offered her.

She and her mom had some savings. But not enough to cover what the medical insurance didn't. This could be the answer to their prayers. This could stop the shadows that were currently residing under her mother's eyes.

The words came out before she could think about it any longer. "I'll see you in an hour."

"Looking forward to it, Ms. Gates."

She glanced at the clock again. Something still didn't sit quite right with her. The apartment at Central Park was gorgeous. But in New York there were dozens of interior designers—competition was tough. She'd never been near a house in the Hamptons before. If that was where Matteo Bianchi owned property he must have a whole range of other contacts.

She smiled. "Mr. Bianchi?"

"Yes, Ms. Gates?"

"How many other interior designers did you call this morning before me?"

There was the briefest hesitation. "Seven."

She let out a laugh. "See you in an hour," she said as she replaced the phone.

Matteo glanced at his watch for the fifth time as he tried not to curse under his breath. It seemed that limousines and New York snowstorms didn't work in partnership together. The car had edged along an inch at a time. Finally, they pulled up outside an apartment. Two seconds later a round figure emerged from the building. She was covered in so many layers he couldn't even see her face. The driver opened the door and Phoebe Gates practically rolled into the car alongside him.

She pushed back her numerous hoods, fixing him with the darkest brown eyes he'd ever seen. She was younger than he'd expected—prettier than he'd expected too, with smooth coffee-colored skin and curls poking out around her face.

She gave him a wide smile as she started unzipping all her jackets. "I think I might have overdone it. I took one look at the snow and put on just about everything I owned."

"I can see that." He couldn't help but smile as she started to emerge from underneath all the layers.

He shook his head as she stripped off a raincoat, a black parka, a zip-up hoody and pushed her mass of curls back from her face. She gave her head a shake. "Wow. It's hot in here."

He kept watching as she folded her arms across her

chest and hitched one knee a little on the seat so she turned to face him. "So, I was number eight, huh?"

He shrugged. "Apparently I picked the wrong time of year to look for an interior designer."

He liked the fact she wasn't afraid to say what she thought. A straight talker. She laughed. "No, I just think you picked the wrong day."

She stared at the snow-covered streets. "So what's the big rush anyhow?"

He settled back into the plush leather seats. "The time is just right."

She wrinkled her nose. It looked as if she might be about to say something when she gave a yell. "Stop the car!"

The driver screeched to a halt, throwing them both forward. "What is it? Did we hit someone?"

She shook her head and shot him a huge grin as she opened the car door. "No. It's my favorite coffee cart. What can I get you?"

Matteo tried not to say the expletives that were circling around his head. "You what? You stopped us like that for *coffee*?"

She stared at him for a second with those big brown eyes, narrowing them for a millisecond as if she were surprised at his reaction. She touched the driver on the shoulder. "You're a macchiato, aren't you?"

The driver blinked in surprise and nodded. She glanced over at the cart. "And a chocolate donut?" He nodded again. She got out of the car and gave her order to the vendor then ducked her head back in and turned to Matteo. She put one finger next to her mouth. "Hmm."

"What?" He was getting annoyed now. New York was starting to get busy with shoppers. It would take around ninety minutes to reach the house and he wanted to get moving as soon as possible.

She gave a half-smile. "I'm trying to work out whether you're a double espresso or an Americano kind of guy."

She ducked back out and spoke quietly to the vendor, who laughed and filled her order. Two minutes later she was in the car and settled back in her seat, handing him a hot paper cup and something in a bag.

She shrugged as he continued to frown. "I get cranky if I don't have coffee in the morning." She shook her head. "And believe me, you won't like me when I'm cranky."

A caramel aroma was drifting over toward him and he watched as she pulled out a raspberry-covered donut, taking a large bite. "Best donuts in New York. Nowhere else comes close."

She nudged him. "Go on. Try yours."

Phoebe Gates was nothing like he'd expected. The last time he'd dealt with an interior designer she'd been all business suits, stiletto heels and clipboards. Her assistant had hung on her every word, constantly taking notes. She'd been abrupt, professional and aloof.

He stared down at the Americano in his hand. Just the way he liked it. And in the paper bag? A regular sugar donut. He hated icing and sprinkles nearly as much as he hated filled donuts.

He frowned. "How did you know?" he asked.

She swallowed her donut and took a sip of her coffee. "How did I know what?"

He held up his Americano and paper bag. "This. How did you know this?"

He was suspicious. People didn't generally surprise him. It wasn't as if she could have done an Internet search to find out what kind of coffee and donut he preferred.

She shrugged again and smiled. "I just know these things." She grinned and tapped her nose. "Interior design. It's all based on observation skills."

Matteo narrowed his gaze. Maybe he'd made a mistake this morning, but by the time he'd reached call number eight he was reaching the desperate stage. In amongst the family feuds of Christmas, the one thing that his overextended Italian family had agreed on was that it was time to get rid of some of the family property. Matteo had agreed to take charge and he intended to get this over with as quickly as possible. He'd thought with the price tag he was offering any interior designer would snap his hand off for the job. Turned out he was wrong. Four of the designers he'd called were on holiday with only an answer-phone message saying calls wouldn't be returning until the new year. Two had answered but refused due to family commitments. One was currently working in Washington. By the time he'd reached Phoebe he just wanted someone to say yes. But then she'd surprised him.

Matteo was used to doing business. He paid a price and a job got done. End of story. So he'd been a little surprised that Phoebe had insisted on seeing the property instead of just agreeing to the job straight away. This was time he really didn't have to spare.

And it wasn't that she seemed unprofessional—that was too harsh. It was just, she seemed so...relaxed.

He'd be paying her a quarter of a million dollars. Was it wrong to expect a little more deference? His insides cringed at the thought. Was he being archaic—or sexist even? In this day and age, neither would be acceptable and both could earn him a slap around the back of the head from his very feisty sister.

She nudged him. "Eat up, or I'll start to think my instincts are off. Now, we've got a bit of time. Give me some history about the house."

Matteo finally took a sip of the coffee. Surprisingly good for a street vendor. He opened his mouth to speak just as his phone rang. He glanced at the caller. Vittore. His brother. Doubtless this would be another fight.

The interruption clarified things in his mind. He turned to Phoebe. "I'm not going to give you any background information on the house." He tried not to look amused. "Let's just see what your instincts tell you." He settled back against the seat as he pressed the phone to his ear.

"Vittore?"

She'd spent the last hour staring out the window at the passing view, desperately wanting to talk. But Mr. Bianchi appeared to conduct most of his business on his phone. Something she'd find depressing on a good day.

Right now, she could be in the middle of Macy's searching for the best bargains.

Maybe the purple coat her mother had admired would be half-price. She could have bought that as a "getting better" present. She'd like to get her mom something to put a smile back on her face. It certainly would be better than spending an hour in forced silence.

The city view had changed rapidly to an even more snow-covered landscape. There was a reason the Hamptons was famous. The popular seaside resort was a historical summer colony on the south fork of Long Island. It featured some of the most luxurious and expensive real estate in all of New York and was regularly featured on TV shows and films.

Phoebe had visited here as a child and a teenager. She'd even spent a semester at the university campus out here and seen exactly how the other half could live. It was almost as if the whole atmosphere changed the further away from the city you got.

She loved New York. She loved the hustle and bustle, she loved the people and she definitely loved living in the city that never slept. But she'd also always loved the Hamptons. Sure, she might not have a billion-dollar bank account. But there was something about this place that made her heartbeat quicken as they passed through one village and hamlet after another. The space. The air. The views. And the houses.

The houses here were *to die for.*

Her stomach gave a little flip-flop as the road stretched ahead of them and they passed one palatial mansion after another. Each one was individual, styled a little differently from its neighbor. Some had been up for more than a hundred years. A few had appeared in the late eighties with a completely modern design that already looked dated.

Mansion spotting was a popular pastime in the Hamptons. A few house builders had obviously decided not to take part in the game and set their homes far back from the road. Phoebe wrinkled her nose. Those people had no sense of fun. What was the point in house spotting if you couldn't even see it?

The car slowed a little and her eyes widened. She was familiar with the surroundings. Anyone who watched TV would be familiar with the surroundings. One of the streets around here was nicknamed Billionaires' Row. Some of the most expensive homes in the US were here.

Phoebe leaned back in the seat and tried to catch her breath. Any minute now they would turn another corner in another direction. She shot a sideways glance at Matteo. He'd told her his home was in Southampton. But she hadn't really thought he'd meant this street. Did people *actually* live here?

The car moved toward the oceanfront, glided through a set of wrought-iron gates, then snaked its way down a long driveway. Sitting in prime position on the oceanfront was one of the biggest houses Phoebe had ever seen.

She couldn't breathe. She actually couldn't breathe. By some miracle Matteo had managed to finish a call and put his phone away.

*Please don't let him expect me to be able to talk right now.*

He seemed unfazed. He glanced upwards—a look of indifference.

To a house like this? Really?

She tried to swallow as there was a little glint of yellow from the top of the house. A curve, covered in snow. Was that an atrium?

The question started to form on her lips then she glimpsed a flash of something else from Matteo. Distaste. Or dislike. She wasn't quite sure which. Really? To a place like this?

*Play it cool.* The words kept repeating over and over in her head. She hadn't been joking when she'd said she liked to see a property before deciding if she would take on a job. But she also liked a chance to meet the client. Interior designers sometimes worked alone. Getting a feel for a job and a client had given her a "Get out of Jail Free" card on a few occasions. Safety always came first and on the odd occasion something just didn't feel right. It had been okay when Jason had been around. He'd always had her back. Clients had taken one look at the strapping ex-Navy pilot and any erroneous thoughts had vanished from their minds. At least that was the way it had always seemed.

But three years ago life had changed in the blink of an eye. Or, more accurately, the stall of two plane engines—something that apparently never happened.

Except to her fiancé. And life would never be the same again.

She'd had to get used to working with no backup plan and part of today had been making sure she felt safe to work for Matteo Bianchi. She shot him a sideways glance. For the most part he seemed like a workaholic typical New York billionaire businessman. An exceptionally *handsome* Italian workaholic businessman.

And that was interesting. Handsome wasn't something she'd noticed in the last three years. Matteo Bianchi had all the traditional attributes of every Italian movie star she'd ever seen on screen. Thick dark hair, deep green eyes, sallow smooth skin and straight white teeth. The only thing that marred his good looks was that permanent frown on his forehead.

She got the distinct impression that he really didn't have time for her. In fact, she got the distinct impression that Matteo Bianchi didn't have time for much of anything.

The car pulled up outside the huge cream-colored mansion and Matteo opened the door straight away. Phoebe fumbled around, trying to select one of her many jackets, finally settling on a red one. She stepped out of the car and looked up at the outside of the house.

The grounds were pristine. She could imagine how manicured the lawns were in summer, even though they were covered in snow right now. The façade was elegant, if a little faded. The double front door was arched and the front of the house lined with mahogany windows covered by internal shutters. Why was a place as beautiful as this all closed up?

If she closed her eyes for a second she could imagine how beautiful this house could be at Christmas. Lights. Trees. Decorations. Instead, it was all closed up like an unwanted present.

Phoebe tilted her head to the side. "Do you only use the house in the summer?"

Matteo shook his head. "We've never really used this house."

"What?" Phoebe spun around and looked at him. "What do you mean, you've never used this house?"

Matteo shook his head and stuck his hands in his pockets. "It's been in the family for a while. But...we've never really stayed here." There was something odd about the way he said that.

Phoebe couldn't help but shake her head. She couldn't get past the fact that this beautiful house was sitting empty—and had done for years.

"Who takes care of it?"

Matteo gave the briefest shake of his head. "I have a caretaker. They come in a few times a year to clean up and maintain the place. Over the years, the electrics, heating and plumbing have all been kept up to date but..." he paused for a second "... I imagine there will be lots of areas in the house that need updating."

Phoebe wrinkled her nose for a second as she stared up at the three-story building with its shuttered windows. "It looks around a hundred years old. Please tell me it's been updated since then."

Matteo gave a nod. "Of course it has. Just not recently."

He pulled a large key from his pocket, along with his phone. As they approached the thick double entrance door he lifted his phone to a panel at the door side. There was a short beep before he turned the key. "Alarm," he said simply before pushing the door open.

Phoebe smiled as she watched him pull the key from the lock. "You put in a digital alarm but didn't put in digital locks?"

He shrugged. There was something so juvenile about it. Like a naughty teenager. "Who says I didn't? I might just be trying to fool you."

It was the first time she'd seen a spark of something. A glimpse of something other than the very busy businessman. A hint of what might lie beneath the surface.

Matteo stood back and she stepped inside the wide entranceway and sucked in a breath.

The air was still all around her. Silent.

But there was something else. Something almost magical.

She held out her hands and spun around. Light flooded in from the open door, allowing her to see the huge curved staircase with intricate iron railing that spiraled up through three floors of the house. Every step she took on the tiled floor echoed upwards to the yellowed glass dome at the top of the house. By the time she stopped spinning and brought her gaze back down to the current floor she finally got a feel for the place. The entranceway was huge.

Matteo was looking at her curiously. There was something odd. He looked uncomfortable. She gave a little stagger and laughed as she put out her hand, grasping onto his sleeve to try and stop her head spinning.

Now she could see all the rooms off the entranceway. Most of them had glass-paneled doors, hinting at what lay beyond. Her heart gave a little flutter.

She'd dreamed of getting the chance to do a house in the Hamptons. It had always been an ambition that she'd hoped to achieve. She just thought it was still at least a few years away. Her fingers were itching to touch this house. To run through every room. To suck in the atmosphere. Trying to appear cool, calm and collected was rapidly slipping from her grasp. Even though Matteo Bianchi was staring her down with that disapproving glare.

She looked to the side again. The room directly to her right was practically calling out to her. "May I?" She gestured with her head.

Matteo stopped glaring and glanced toward the room. A furrow lined his brow. "Actually, I want you to let me know what your instincts tell you."

It was the way he said it. The tone. And the way the glare in his eyes had been replaced by a kind of mischievous twinkle. He was testing her. Or teasing her.

She tilted her chin upwards. Matteo Bianchi had no idea who he was dealing with. She met his green gaze straight on. "You know you're being unfair—but that's fine." She held up her hands. "I've already told you I think the house is around a hundred years old." She wrinkled her nose. "About twenty thousand square meters? Maybe around eight or nine bedrooms? Probably four or five bathrooms or half-baths. I expect two or three formal rooms. I expect a dining room, a large kitchen, laundry, study and a basement and wine cellar." She put her hand on her chest. "And I'm hoping there are *exceptional* views over Mecox Bay from the rear of the property. Am I getting close? Can I actually get in to see the main sitting room?"

Matteo gave a nod toward the door. Phoebe didn't wait another second; she was through that door in a flash.

It was like a moment out of time. She blinked as a memory of a movie she'd watched flooded through her senses. The hero and heroine had flitted back and forth between modern day and fifty years before. Phoebe felt as if she were currently standing by their side.

She couldn't help but touch. Tiny slivers of bright light tried to edge their way around the shutters. Phoebe didn't wait, she walked over to the nearest set and gave them a tug.

Nothing happened.

She tried again. This time there was a creak. A squeak. She slid her hand up the side, checking for any extra latches or bolts. Once she was sure there were none, she pulled with all her might.

Two seconds later she was flat on her back on the carpet as the winter's day light filled the room. She laughed as Matteo moved above her, holding his hand out toward her. "Are you okay?"

She kept laughing and stayed on the floor, shaking her head. "I'm still dreaming, aren't I? Because this dream just seems to get kookier by the minute."

He frowned, staring at his outstretched hand, as if he were trying to figure out what was wrong with it. "I have no idea what you mean."

"Oh, come on." She leaned up on her hand, still staying on the carpet as her gaze swept across the room. "You phoned me this morning and offered me a quarter of a million dollars for a few weeks' work, dressing a home in the Hamptons. Every designer's dream. Then you bring me here. The house to end *all* houses." She was shaking her head again now. "Then, we come in, and it's a time warp. A perfect time warp." She held up her hand as her eyes tried not to goggle in amazement at the contents of the room.

"I still don't know what you mean."

She pushed herself up onto her bottom. "This place. This furniture."

Matteo shook his head. "I know. I know. Everything will need replacing it's all so out of date. Don't worry. I'll give you a credit card with no limit. You can buy whatever you need to dress the house." He waved his hand. "As long as you keep receipts, of course."

"Are you crazy?" She couldn't believe what he was saying. She reached out and touched the chair next to her. "This stuff is pristine. Perfect. People would pay an absolute fortune for things like this. And I won't need to. Because it's all here. Matteo, don't you realize how fantastic this place already is?"

He was looking at her as if she were out of her mind.

She grabbed his hand and pulled herself up as she paced quickly around the room. "This—this is why I think I'm still dreaming. See this? This nineteen-fifties chair? I paid over a thousand dollars for one of these last time I dressed a home. You've got six." She touched the L-shaped sofa in the corner. "I might get this reupholstered but the style and shape is just fabulous."

Her heart skittered across her chest as she took in all the fixtures and fittings. The lamps, the shades, the telephone, the vases. She shook her head again as she murmured, "It's like interior design heaven. That's why this must be a dream. Things like this don't happen to me."

She spun around and gasped. Matteo had walked right up behind her. He was closer than expected and was watching her with the most curious expression on his face. Her dream from earlier had been filled by Hugh Jackman. If she were still dreaming, wouldn't Hugh be the man that had brought her to this house instead of Matteo Bianchi?

"Pinch me," she said firmly.

"What?"

"Pinch me. I have to know this isn't a dream."

He was right in front of her. Staring her down with those green eyes. Part of him looked amused, part of him looked annoyed. Or maybe she was just misreading him. The hint of aftershave was distracting her. It was subtle. She'd never smelt it before. Amber, musk and oak moss. People didn't realize that interior designers knew that scent was everything. Half of all homes sold on scent alone.

"Go on," she urged. "Just do it."

He pulled an exasperated face then lifted his hand to her arm.

"Yeowwww!" She jumped backwards, rubbing her wrist. "Okay, then. Turns out I'm definitely awake." She shot him a suspicious glance. "You've got sisters, haven't you? Or *a* sister."

"How on earth do you know that?"

"Believe me." She kept rubbing her smarting wrist. "A girl can tell."

He stared at her curiously for a second. "And for the record, I have one sister. One is enough."

She took a deep breath. This was it. This was where she found out if this really was the dream job. "Tell me, is every room as good as this one?"

Matteo raised his eyebrows. "You mean, is every room in the same kind of time warp as this one? Oh, I can guarantee that, Phoebe." He was looking at her as if he couldn't quite understand why she thought this was a good thing. But Phoebe was off. Tearing through the next few rooms of the house to check them out. A dining room. A huge kitchen. A laundry room. Another sitting room. A study. Two bathrooms—they might need a little work. And a phenomenal room at the back of the house with windows and glass doors that looked out over Mecox Bay.

Matteo stayed behind her, following her from room to room. "Phoebe... Ms. Gates. Does this mean you'll take the job?"

She could hardly speak. Room after room, there were so many thoughts clambering in her brain about how gorgeous she could make this place that she could hardly form words. Her dream job. The job that could change her whole career. A chance to pay off her mother's medical bills. A chance to move forward. A chance to pull herself out of the fog that had hung around her for the last few years.

"Phoebe." His voice grew sharp and he gave her arm a pull, tugging her around to face him. Her hands rested on his upper arms. She couldn't help herself. She almost wanted to give him a kiss on the cheek. She let out a laugh.

"Do I want the job? Hell, yes. Now I've seen it, this place is mine. Matteo, I'm going to do such a good job, you're never going to want to let me go."

It was the briefest of seconds. A wash of sadness seemed to sweep his face. A whole host of something she really didn't understand. But as soon as it had appeared, the shutters came down in his eyes again. Matteo Bianchi had the perfect mask. The perfect face for business.

The edges of his lips curved upwards. For the first

time since she'd met him, the tension in his shoulders actually looked as if it disappeared a little. "Phoebe, quarter of a million dollars for four weeks' work, and I *will* let you go."

# CHAPTER TWO

FOR THE FIRST time in years Phoebe actually felt lucky. It was a strange concept. Unfamiliar.

Lucky had been something she'd taken for granted for so long. Then Jason, her fiancé, had been killed in a freak flying accident. They'd only just got engaged and started to make plans for the future. All of those things wiped out in the blink of an eye—or the failure of two engines at once. She still couldn't even think about it. But Phoebe hadn't needed therapy. She was strong. Or so she'd thought. She'd been devastated to lose her fiancé, but she'd picked herself up and continued to go through the motions.

Then her mother had got sick. Cancer. Surgery. Chemotherapy. Radiotherapy. And a million scans. Phoebe had been determined to take her to every appointment, every treatment. And she had. Running herself into the ground while she did it. Forgetting to eat. Forgetting to sleep. And eventually having to hit therapy. Because she *did* need it. She just hadn't wanted to acknowledge it.

It was just lately that she'd felt as if she was starting to come out the tunnel she'd been hiding in. Her mom was doing better. They only had to settle the medical bills now. But work had picked up. The apartment near Central Park had been a real coup for her. But this?

This was the icing on the cake. Better than that. This was the sugar on the sprinkles, on the chocolate, on the icing on the cake.

She wasn't the slightest bit perturbed by Matteo telling her he'd let her go. She'd been on a high. She still was. He was somewhere behind her as she rushed from room to room, throwing open shutters and taking photo after photo with her phone. Occasionally she stopped to make a few notes. But only for a second. The essence of this house was invading her senses. The myriad of bedrooms. The bathrooms that could do with a little updating. The totally and completely gorgeous central yellow glass dome. And the kitchen. She could do so much with the kitchen that she almost wanted to start this very second.

Matteo's mood seemed a little odd. Almost sedated if that made sense. She got the distinct impression he didn't want to be here at all. It was almost as if he didn't even like the place.

By the time she returned to the main room Matteo was back on his phone. She should probably be paying some kind of deference to him since he was going to be paying her enormous salary, but she was far too excited for all that.

She walked straight over to him. "I still hurt from where you pinched me."

He was mid conversation and raised one eyebrow at her. After the briefest of pauses he pulled the phone away from his ear. "I'm in the middle of something."

"So am I. And you spent all the time in the car on the phone." There was something about this guy. He was obviously far too wealthy for words. He was clearly a workaholic. But there was just something in his eyes. He liked someone to challenge him. He was amused by her. And somehow she already knew she wanted to earn his respect. If that meant demanding his attention, then she could do that.

He glanced at his phone, but didn't continue with that conversation. The edges of his lips curved again. "You asked me to pinch you. I only did what you asked." There was a cheeky hint in his tone.

"When do I get to meet your sister? I can already tell that I'll be bruised from that pinch and I want to compare notes with her."

He paused and disconnected the call. "The very *last* person I'm introducing you to is my sister. Brianna is even crazier than you are. You'd be a lethal combination."

Phoebe folded her arms across her chest. "Brianna. I like the sound of her." She nodded her head. "You don't need to worry. I'll meet her. And I promise to be on my best behavior." She held up her hands. "Now, the house. I have so many ideas. So many plans. Let's walk through and I'll talk you through them. I can draw up something more formal in a few days. I'll need to check if any of the people I regularly use are free to help out." She raised her eyebrows. "For some people, this is the holiday season."

Matteo frowned and shook his head. "No, no. I'll leave all that to you. I don't need to see plans. I don't need to know your thoughts. I can give you contacts for teams to assist."

Phoebe stood back a little and looked at him incredulously. "You are joking, right?"

He gave her a stern stare. "Why would I be joking?"

She couldn't believe what she was hearing. "Mr. Bianchi, usually clients want consulted on the plans, the overall look for their home. Often they want consulted on any major purchases." She couldn't help but frown. "People are generally passionate about how their homes are marketed—what they look like. They usually want to be involved to ensure they get the best price possible."

Matteo gave an ironic smile. "I take it you're used to clients who generally care about their homes—and the price they achieve. I care about neither. I just want this place off my hands." As he finished his phone started ringing again and he strode out of the room, pressing it to his ear, leaving Phoebe wondering whether to laugh or cry. It was clear the conversation was over.

He'd picked a crazy woman. At one point he'd thought Phoebe Gates would start cartwheeling around the place. She was barely managing to keep her excitement simmering beneath the surface. Her joy at having this job seemed to emanate from every pore in her body.

That actually made a tiny little part of him happy. There was something nice about her enthusiasm and straightforwardness. In his line of business he was used to fake smiles and poker faces; somehow he didn't think Phoebe Gates would know how to do either one.

But Phoebe obviously had very different ideas from him. She'd thrown open shutters and flooded this dusty old house with light, her face brightening as she'd practically run from room to room. He was surprised that she loved the ancient furniture and fittings. He'd been sure any interior designer would just skip the contents of the house and redecorate the place from top to bottom. Phoebe had obviously decided to take a different tack.

He'd reached the kitchen by now and let out a long sigh. The sooner he got out of here, the better. He only had one association with this house. And it was one he had no intention of revisiting.

He stared around the kitchen for a few seconds as something flashed through his brain. A long-forgotten memory. His mother. Those memories were so fleeting. So scant.

Her dark hair and bright eyes. Dressed in a swirling red dress. She'd been excited. Just the way that Phoebe was. Full of ideas and plans for what she could do to the house. The house they'd just bought that was stuck in a time warp. It had been owned by an elderly actress who had died a few months earlier. His mother could hardly wait to bring it up to modern-day living.

He remembered his father leaning against the double sink and folding his arms, smiling and watching Matteo's mother the way he'd always watched her—with love and adoration in his eyes.

When Matteo blinked, the memory was gone. He inhaled deeply and leaned back against the sink—just the way his father had. Was the memory even real? He would only have been around five when they stayed here for a few weeks. Brianna was only a few weeks old and Vittore around three.

But everything changed. The house was boarded up and they moved with their father back to Rome, flitting between the capital and an apartment in New York City, then London for a while. The house in the Hamptons was never mentioned. Ignored.

Too many painful memories. It was only now, thirty years later, the family had decided it was time to sell.

Phoebe floated into the kitchen. Literally, floated. Her smile spread from ear to ear, showing off her straight white teeth and enhancing her glowing coffee-colored skin. Her hair bounced as she walked, tight corkscrew curls resting on her shoulders. There was something about her. An aura. She made him want to smile. He couldn't even remember the last time he'd felt like that. For a few seconds she'd even made him forget where he actually was. But the truth was, he just couldn't shake the sense of this place. The dark memories. The secrets he'd learned to keep. The ones that kept him locked away.

Phoebe moved in front of him. She'd shed more layers. Now he could see the way her green fine-knit jumper and fitted black trousers clung to her curves. Many of the women Matteo came across in New York were skeletally thin. It was a look he'd never appreciated. Italian men much preferred women with curves— and Phoebe wore them well.

Her perfume drifted up around him as she fixed her chocolate-brown eyes on him. She paused for a second, with an amused expression on her face. It was clear she was contemplating how to phrase her words.

"Ms. Gates?" he prompted.

She gave a nod. "How about we settle on Phoebe and Matteo? I think that might make things a bit easier. After all, we will be seeing a lot of each other."

There was a sparkle in her eyes.

He slid his hand into his pocket and pulled out a credit card. "I'm not sure that will be necessary. But I'm happy to call you Phoebe if that's what you prefer."

She took the credit card without a glance, merely sliding it into the back pocket of her trousers.

"We need to talk about this place, Matteo. We need to discuss my plans." It was clear that persistence was one of her traits.

He was curt. "No. We don't."

He turned on his heel and walked out of the kitchen, heading in the direction of the front door. In the space of few seconds it almost felt as if the walls were closing in around him.

The cool air almost bit into his skin as he stepped outside and he blinked at the brightness. He hadn't realized quite how blinkered the house had been.

His phone started ringing. He pulled it from his pocket—Brianna. He might have guessed. They were closer than some families. He spoke to both his brother and sister a few times a day. A few female companions in the past had commented on it—finding it strange. But Matteo had never cared for other people's opinions on his family. They hadn't lived his life, they didn't know that he and his siblings were the glue that held their splintered family together.

"Did you get one?" Brianna was speaking rapidly in Italian. She was probably doing ten things at once.

"I did."

"And? Are they good?"

Was Phoebe Gates good? He didn't really know. He'd called her both on a whim and out of desperation. Captain Monaghan had been one of the most interesting men Matteo had ever had the pleasure of meeting. But his apartment had been a cluttered, claustrophobic mess. Rudy Monaghan was clearly a hoarder. He'd sailed the seven seas and collected just about everything he'd ever seen.

Matteo had never met Phoebe, but Rudy had been full of praise for the beautiful, enthusiastic and, most importantly, respectful interior designer that he'd hired. The crew she'd hired to assist her had been given very clear instructions. Carefully pack up everything without a yellow sticker. Walls had been painted, windows shined, pictures moved and rehung. She'd stripped the place bare but kept its heart and essence.

No, she'd kept Rudy Monaghan's heart and essence.

Matteo had dropped in one evening just before he knew Rudy was due to move out and been struck by the enormity of the changes. Rudy had been sitting in his wooden rocking chair, his genuine ancient ship's wheel still next to him, bathed in the orange setting sun, watching the view of Central Park. That sight would stay with Matteo forever.

He took a deep breath. Now he remembered the transformation he almost wished he'd called Phoebe first. He couldn't help but smile. He could just imagine how she'd have been if he'd called her at seven instead of eight. "They're not good, Brianna," he said deliberately.

"What?" she shrieked from somewhere in New York.

"They're great. *She's* great."

There was silence for a few seconds. He waited for the tirade of abuse from his sister for momentarily teasing her but it didn't come.

"Matteo, who is *she*?"

There was something about his sister's tone. Her curiosity. He instantly felt a prickle down his spine. Brianna was nosey. Brianna was beyond nosey. He probably shouldn't have said anything at all.

He kept his voice brisk. "She's Phoebe Gates. Remember Rudy's apartment at Central Park? She did that one. She'll do a good job for us."

He could almost hear the cogs and whirrs of Brianna's brain. "Yeah, I remember the apartment at Central Park. It ended up as part of a bidding war, didn't it?"

"Well, if that's what you heard, it must be true."

"So, we know Ms. Gates can dress an apartment— but can she dress a Hampton house?"

She hadn't said the words out loud but the implication was clear. An apartment at Central Park was big. A house in the Hamptons was in a whole other league.

"Have a little faith in your brother, Brianna."

There was a loud sigh at the end of the phone. "I have a lot of faith in my brother. Both my brothers." There was a pause for a second. Matteo had kept walking. The fresh air was calling to him, along with the spectacularly white snow. The tone of her voice softened. "How are you?"

He didn't answer. Cold air was filling his lungs, letting his heart race a little quicker and letting him shake off the cobwebs.

It was hard to explain. The only other people to have walked in his shoes were Vittore and Brianna. No one else would ever understand. He wouldn't expect them to. He wouldn't want them to. And the truth was, Vittore and Brianna didn't understand entirely either—because he didn't want them to. He was oldest. It was his job to guard his younger brother and sister.

"Matteo?" Her voice was soft, almost a whisper.

Matteo closed his eyes. "I'm fine, Brianna. Of course, I'm fine. It's just this place. You know that. I'm going to leave everything in Phoebe's hands. She doesn't see this place the way we do. She loves it. She thinks it's great. She…she has the ability to dress it and make it sell. That's all that we need."

He could almost hear the shake in her voice. "Is it?"

It was as if the cold air penetrated every part of him. He wouldn't go there. He wouldn't have the conversation that his sister sometimes pushed him toward. He'd learned how to deal with it over the years. It was as if he owned his own set of black shutters. Push him so far and he would just slam them shut. "Goodbye, Brianna," he said smartly as he finished the call.

* * *

Phoebe was sitting on the curved staircase. Her feet had actually started to follow him out of the kitchen, then her instincts had kicked in and told her not to. Told her to give him a little space.

Mr. Bianchi was more than a little temperamental. Was this an Italian trait?

She sighed and closed her eyes, trying to breathe in the essence of this beautiful home. Her brain instantly took her to the place she wanted to be. Right now she was recreating her own favorite musical and was tap dancing up and down these stairs in a bouffant yellow dress. She just hadn't decided who her imaginary leading man was yet. A twinge of guilt set in.

For the first year after Jason's death he'd been the main feature of every dream she'd had. But for the last year, several movie stars had started to creep in and take over. In a way, it had been a relief to stop waking up with her heart in her throat. That horrible little millisecond of time—the briefest of moments—where she thought everything was just the same, Jason was still here, her mom wasn't sick yet and then, she remembered.

And that overwhelming colossal black wave swamped back on top of her, every morning, making her relive every moment and making her want to be sick all over her bed. It took months for that to fade. Months to wake up to the reality that was her life.

But every time she felt relief that didn't happen anymore, guilt pricked at her conscience.

She took a deep breath and pressed her hands on the cool marble stairs, letting her eyes flicker open. She could imagine the beautiful women and men who'd walked these steps. The hopes, dreams and fantasy life-styles. Things that were all so far out of her reach.

She shook her head and smiled. Jealousy had never been a Phoebe trait. She loved that this place had history. She loved that it had been captured in time. She would probably never get a chance like this again. She just had to know what to keep to help capture the story, and know what to replace to make this home still seem appealing to a modern-day buyer.

The color palette here was unreal. She'd found an avocado bathroom. That would definitely have to be dealt with. But so much else just needed tweaks. She pulled out her phone and flicked through her contacts as she breathed in deeply. There was a bit of an odor. A tang that frequently featured in houses that hadn't really been lived in for a number of years.

Smell was so much. But she could deal with that. Carpets, drapes and upholstery could all be replaced. But she wasn't sure she would change the style. So much of it was perfect.

She pressed a familiar number of her phone. It answered on the second ring.

"Hello, baby girl."

"Hi, Momma. I've got news."

"Are you at the sales? What did you buy?"

Phoebe laughed. "No, Momma. I'm in a whole different place." She looked around as her heart gave a little jump. "I just want you to know that in a few weeks, the medical bills won't be a problem."

There was a sharp intake of breath. Her mother's voice was panicked. "Baby girl, what have you done?"

It didn't matter she was twenty-seven. It didn't matter that she had her own place and her own life. She would always be her mother's baby.

She laughed. "I haven't done anything, Momma. I just got the job of my dreams. And it pays more than I could ever have hoped for."

Her mother's tone hadn't changed from panic. "Phoebe, what kind of job is this?"

Phoebe shook her head. "It's exactly the kind of job I do every day. But this house…" she pressed one hand to her chest and breathed in, as if saying it made everything real "…it's in the Hamptons."

"What?" Her mother's voice came out as a squeak.

"Yes," Phoebe said quickly. "I got a call this morning." She lowered her voice to a whisper. "A quarter of a million dollars if I can work over the next four weeks and redress this house."

"How much?" This time it wasn't a squeak. This time it was more like a shriek.

But Phoebe didn't get a chance to answer. "Who is this person with a house in the Hamptons? Are they a criminal? Who have you got mixed up with? How did they find out about you?"

Phoebe shook her head. "Calm down, Mom. They know Rudy. That's how they know about me. They liked the work I did on his apartment. That's how I got this job. I came out to see the house this morning and…" she tried to steady her thoughts "…it's a dream come true. It's like walking into a fifties TV show. The whole place, it's just…epic." She laughed at using such a juvenile word, but nothing else seemed to come close.

Her mother cut straight to the chase. "Are you safe? Have you met these folks? Are they good people?"

"They're an Italian family."

Her mother's voice lowered to a hushed tone. "Are they part of the mob?"

Phoebe choked. "What? No? Don't be ridiculous.

They've had this house for a while. It's just time to sell it." But something prickled. Matteo hadn't been exactly straight with her. The timing did seem a little off. Exactly how old was he? "And yes. I'm safe. Matteo is a bit buttoned up. He's a businessman. One of those high-flyer types. But he seems sincere. And I think I'm going to love doing this job. This could be it. This could be the one. It will pay off the bills and maybe put me on the map."

There was a few seconds' silence. "Then go nail it. I love you, baby girl."

Phoebe smiled as she pushed her phone back in her pocket and stood up again. The front door was wide open to the world, letting in an icy blast. Matteo must have gone outside.

She'd left her jacket somewhere she couldn't entirely remember, so she crossed her hands over her body as she walked outside.

Matteo had that strange, dark expression on his face again. The one where he didn't really answer any questions. But Phoebe was determined. She might have the credit card, but she wanted to do the best job in the world. Her career could depend on it. Her bank balance certainly did. And for that, she needed a bit more information.

"Matteo?" He spun around, frowning. It seemed to be his default expression.

She walked up to him, close enough to let his body block out the swirling wind coming from Mecox Bay. "You haven't been entirely straight with me."

The furrow on his brow deepened. "What do you mean?"

She gave a gentle smile. "Unless, of course, you're a modern-day Peter Pan."

Now he just looked confused. "What?"

She inched a little closer. Probably more than she meant to. Her hair was getting caught by the wind, blowing her springy curls in front of her eyes. "The timing doesn't fit," she said quietly. "I'm trying to work out why you lived in a nineteen-fifties-style house." She tilted her head to the side as she studied him a little harder. "Don't get me wrong—I love it. But you don't look in your sixties. Maybe you've discovered some secret cream the rest of the world just needs to find?"

She could almost see the penny drop. She expected him to smile. But he didn't. Instead she could almost feel the wave of sadness. His voice was quiet. "We bought the house in the late eighties when I was a child. It belonged to some ageing starlet who had moved into it in the nineteen-fifties and not redecorated since. My parents had plans to redecorate the whole house. But... things changed. We only stayed here a few weeks. My father's business meant we had to go to Rome, then London for a while. When we came back to New York, we had a few other properties that were ready to move into as a family."

He said the words as if something were squirming in his chest, and his bright green eyes only met her gaze for the most fleeting of seconds.

It wasn't a lie. But it didn't feel like the truth. *Trust your instincts,* the voice in her head said. She wasn't getting the fight-or-flight feeling. There was more to this. But whatever it was—it wasn't enough to walk away from her dream job. A chance to pay the medical bills and possibly make her mark on the Hamptons.

"You've moved around a lot. The family business— what kind of business are you in?"

The fleeting mob reference from her mother was momentarily playing on her mind.

"I'm Italian." He raised his eyebrows. "We're in the wine business."

"You own vineyards?"

Matteo gave a tight smile "We own seventeen vineyards in Italy. Sixteen in Spain, fourteen in California, and several in Portugal."

"Wow. That's a lot of wine." She rolled her eyes. "I guess I don't need to worry about stocking the cellar, then."

He gave a brief shake of his head. "Let me deal with that."

She nodded. "Are you in a hurry to leave? I'd like to stay. I'd like to spend as much time as I can here, to get a feel for the place. I need to go over every room in detail, and I need to call contacts to check availability, and see what I can achieve over the next four weeks."

She wanted him to know she was serious. She wanted him to know that this was important to her.

He glanced toward the limousine then shook his head. "Keep the car, it's fine. I can arrange another form of transport." His gaze actually met hers. This time there was something else. Something that made her heart swell a little. Respect?

She turned to go back to the house but his voice carried on the wind toward her.

"Ms. Gates? I trust you. I know you'll do a good job."

Her footsteps froze, but by the time she turned back around he already had the phone pressed against his ear again.

Had she imagined it?

# CHAPTER THREE

THE PHOTOGRAPHS OF how the house looked right now were printed. She'd spent the last two days sketching her new vision for the house. The avocado bathroom was already gone. Some things didn't need to wait. She'd learned very quickly that Matteo really didn't want to take her calls.

He'd given her a credit card that she hadn't used yet. But working with contractors was different. She'd had to agree the price for a few jobs—and at this time of year—and for a house in the Hamptons—some of the prices quoted had been exorbitant. Any good interior designer would run those past her employer and that was all Phoebe was doing. Though Matteo wasn't really interested in contractor prices. So far, he'd said yes to anything without so much as a blink.

Her biggest expense for the house was going to be fabric. She wanted new drapes for just about every room, and lots of the signature pieces reupholstered. And good quality fabric was *not* cheap. Which was why she standing in one of the most prestigious, well-stocked warehouses on the outskirts of New York.

But this place didn't like to waste time. The assistant assigned to her held out her hand. "We'll just put your credit card on file to ease things along."

She got it. She did. The assistant didn't want to spend the next four hours helping Phoebe find everything she wanted, only to have the credit card declined at the end.

Phoebe slipped the black card from her purse and handed it over. She had a long list of fabrics she wanted to find. A color palette already existed in her head, but would she find a match in this warehouse? That was always the danger of getting too carried away with one idea. Sometimes color trends and seasons just didn't match. So, she'd prepared some sketches with one set of colors, and prepared some more as a backup plan.

The assistant walked back over and held out the credit card as if it had the plague. "I'm sorry. Your credit line doesn't seem to be approved. Do you have another card you can use?"

Phoebe felt her cheeks flush. She did have another credit card. Unfortunately it was maxed out with her mother's medical expenses, and the amount of money she'd likely spend in here today could never be covered by the small amount of money in her current account.

She'd had a bad start already this morning, tangling herself up in her sheets when the alarm had gone off, falling out of bed and catching the side of her cheek on the bedside cabinet. She was just hoping it wouldn't bruise.

"Give me a minute," she said, trying not to seem embarrassed. She pulled her phone from her pocket and dialed Matteo's number. *Please answer.* She didn't want to have to walk out of here after presenting a dud card. She'd never be able to show her face again, and this place was every interior designer's dream. She couldn't afford to have a bad rep in here.

"Matteo Bianchi." His reply was curt. But he couldn't hide that wonderful Italian accent that sent tingles down to her toes. Every time she called she forgot about it and spent the first few seconds of their conversation lost in a little fog.

Right now she didn't have time for a fog. She cut to the chase. "Matteo, the credit card you gave me isn't working."

It took a few seconds for a reply. She could almost picture him staring at the name on the phone. How many people did he give credit cards to? "Phoebe?"

"Of course, Phoebe. Who else would it be?"

"Where are you?"

"I'm at a warehouse on the outskirts of New York. I need to buy fabrics, leathers—a whole host of things for the house." She lowered her voice as the assistant glared at her, obviously labeling her as a time waster. "This place is expensive and you've given me a limited amount of time."

"Let me speak to them."

Phoebe sighed and handed over the phone to the assistant, pacing at the side while Matteo obviously had a curt conversation with her.

"No, Mr. Bianchi. Your personal guarantee is not good enough."

Phoebe tried not to smile at the thought of Matteo's response.

"You'll need to speak to your credit card provider."

The assistant rolled her eyes and held the phone a little away from her ear. Phoebe walked over to some large rolls of fabric and started to study them closely.

"The only way around things is for you to come down yourself and bring your alternative credit card. No, we can't just take the number over the phone. We need to see the card, along with your signature." The woman let out a sigh. "Yes. That's the only way."

She replaced the receiver and gave Phoebe a fake smile. "Mr...Bianchi will be with you shortly."

"Great," Phoebe muttered as every little hair on her arm stood on end. Just what she needed, an angry Matteo.

This day was getting better and better.

Matteo tried not to curse at his driver as they took another wrong turn. It seemed the sat-nav had decided not to work properly and this industrial estate had dozens of identical giant warehouses, along with no map at the entrance to the site.

He was annoyed at himself. He was sure he'd activated that card. But in amongst the family discussions at Christmas it was possible he might have forgotten. And he should have kept a copy of Phoebe's signature on record so it could be verified, but visiting the house in the Hamptons again had scrambled his normally precise brain.

He hadn't expected to be hit by the wave of emotions. How much could a five-year-old really remember? But being back in that environment had swamped him in a way he hadn't expected. And having the unconventional Ms. Gates with him had probably been a blessing. She'd distracted him from too much melancholy. Too much emotion. Too many flashbacks he hadn't counted on.

And now? Now, more than ever he just wanted to finalize the sale of the house. In his head this was the only way to push all these feelings back into the box where they belonged.

"It's this one," said the driver as they pulled up.

Matteo gave a nod and stepped outside onto the frost-covered ground. This shouldn't take long. He had work to do.

The warehouse was massive, cavernous with an echo that seemed to reverberate all around him. But the first thing that struck him was how methodical everything seemed. The fabrics were stored by color, stacked for what seemed like miles. Large trolleys were pushed around by assistants, who guided customers around the warehouse.

He could pick Phoebe out easily. She was wearing a bright pink coat with matching furry hat and leather gloves. She gave him a rueful smile as he approached. "You might have checked the card worked before you gave it to me."

He tried to hide his annoyance as he pulled his own from his wallet. He glanced around him. "What do you need me to pay for?"

Phoebe wrinkled her nose. "Nothing...yet. They wouldn't let me start shopping until I had a credit line."

"You mean you haven't even started shopping?" His voice echoed louder than expected.

Phoebe pulled back a little and gave him a frown. "No. I haven't started."

Matteo strode over to the counter and thrust his card in front of one of the assistants. "Here's my card. Can you take the details, so I can leave?"

The assistant gave him an icy stare. It was clear she didn't like being treated so dismissively. She gave him a haughty smile. "I can take your details now—but you have to produce your card and match the signature to complete your purchases." She gestured to the side. "You can always get yourself a coffee while your wife shops."

Matteo started. She thought Phoebe was his wife? He stared at the boutique-style coffee shop housed inside

the warehouse. While the smell of coffee was tempt-
ing, the waste of his time was not.

He turned to face Phoebe, who was standing open-
mouthed. She must have heard the comment too. "How
long will this take?"

Phoebe cringed. It was clear she didn't want to give
the true answer.

He flung up his hands. "How long does it take to buy
some fabric and some vases?"

Phoebe's face became pinched. She strode over to
the nearest large trolley and turned to one of the assistants. "Are we ready to get started?"

Matteo tried not to let his mouth bounce off the
floor. She'd just completely ignored him. Part of him
was amused, part of him was annoyed. She had a huge
sketch pad balanced on top of the trolley. She tossed her
hair over her shoulder and pointed to her first sketch.
"This is the color palette I'm interested in. Can we go
in that direction please?"

Matteo's curiosity was piqued. Didn't every interior
designer just paint houses in white or shades of cream?

The assistant looked positively excited. "Oh, that's
so unusual." She leaned over the sketch. "And I love
this color palette. I'm sure we can find you some perfect fabrics that will suit."

The assistant started pushing the trolley in one direction. Matteo glanced at the coffee shop. He could
sit there. But as he glanced at his phone he could see
the signal here wasn't great—probably why the sat-
nav hadn't functioned. How much work would he really get done?

Before he could think again, his feet started to follow
the trolley and Phoebe and the assistant. They moved
past the white and cream rolls of fabrics, away from

the brighter reds and oranges and toward the back of the warehouse. Whatever color she'd chosen it clearly wasn't the most popular. His stomach gave a little twist. Maybe he should be showing more interest?

He walked quickly, catching up with them and leaning directly over Phoebe's shoulder. He blinked. Then nearly stumbled, reaching out and catching onto the handle of the trolley.

"Yellow?" he asked Phoebe.

She gave him a firm stare. "Oh, you've joined us." Her tone reminded him of a headmistress.

His eyes couldn't move from the sketch. It was more than good. A hand drawing that had captured the whole breadth of the main room, gently shaded with coloring pencils in shades of gray, yellow, pale blue and cream.

It was beautiful. Exquisite even. But yellow was a color he'd never really seen at any other houses for sale. It did seem unusual.

Phoebe pointed to the sketch. "I always like to choose a color palette—a theme—for any house that I dress." She pressed her lips together for a second. "While it makes sense to use a neutral background color, I always have to pick some secondary colors to highlight parts of the interior." She turned to face Matteo. "In your case, what other color could I choose? The yellow dome above the atrium is really the focal point of the house. It bathes the whole house in that magical yellow light. Yellow seems the natural color to pick out. I've teamed it with some shades of pale blue, gray and cream." She flicked the first page to show him a sketch of one of the bathrooms, followed by one of the bedrooms, then the back room that looked out over Mecox Bay.

The attention to detail was extraordinary. The main room still had the same nineteen-fifties sofa, but this time it was covered in what looked like pale blue leather. The drapes were striped in shades of pale yellow and gray. There was a sleek gray rug on the large wooden floor. All of this was dressed with bursts of bright yellow. A sunflower portrait on the wall. A few cushions, and a bright yellow table lamp. "You did all these in the last few days?"

Phoebe nodded. "Of course, I did. This is what I do." She looked at him hesitantly. "I did do an alternative color scheme if you'd prefer." She flicked to the back of the sketch pad where she had the same room sketches, but this time with white, beige and splashes of orange. It was more abstract, but more traditional. The kind of thing he was used to seeing in other houses. He gave a little shudder. Even though the yellow was a surprise, it was clear the more stark colors wouldn't complement the house as much. The yellow gave the house a warmth that made it much more welcoming.

"What do you think?" She sounded a little nervous.

He nodded. "I think it's good. You're right about the yellow." He glanced around. "I just hope you can find what you need—and quickly," he added with a murmur.

They turned a corner in the warehouse and Matteo stopped walking. The shades of yellow were overwhelming. And it seemed this warehouse didn't just keep the same color fabrics together. No, across wide display units there were rugs, bedding, vases, lamps and ornaments all in complementary shades.

Phoebe let out a little gasp and walked away, running her hand over a large dark gray rug, with pale yellow circles. "This is perfect," she said, nodding to the assistant. "We'll take it." She moved without drawing breath over to a wooden cabinet with upright rolls of fabric. She pointed to a pale gray and yellow stripe. "I'll have this one. And the one next to it with duck-egg blue and yellow." She turned to face the wooden cabinets behind them. "I also want the pale yellow and cream pattern over there. It will be perfect for the master bedroom."

Her bright pink coat swirled around her as she picked up bedding, ornaments, vases and lamp shades in a whole variety of shades of gray, blue and yellow. When she'd finished loading the trolley she waved Matteo over to another part of the warehouse. "Let's pick some prints," she said as she started flicking through a sheaf of prints held behind plastic frames.

The colors stood out, but it was clear that Matteo didn't have Phoebe's designer eye. She let out a little squeal as she found a yellow sunflower similar to the one she'd sketched in her designs. She flicked on and found a gold *broderie anglaise* design, some pale blue cornflowers, and a beautiful beach scene with a turquoise sea.

By now, it seemed that she'd forgotten her apparent bad mood with Matteo. Every single time she found another item she couldn't stop talking. "This is perfect for the back room." She was holding a swirling glass ornament in shades of pale blue. "I can see it sitting on a table with a view of Mecox Bay in the background." She turned and pointed at a pale blue patterned fabric. "And this will frame the windows in the kitchen perfectly. It's just the right shade of blue. And look at these ceramic jugs in blue and cream. They'll be perfect to dress the kitchen." She turned to face him. "Did I tell you I'm getting the sink replaced? There's going to be dual sinks, deep white Belfast sinks, with a thick dark wood countertop. That, along with some replacement handles, will set the kitchen off perfectly. Oh, and I've ordered some new appliances." She glanced in her diary. "They arrive tomorrow. We'll need to have a chat about access."

Matteo nodded. She was like a firecracker. Once she started, she just couldn't stop. The enthusiasm just brimmed out of her. Part of him wished he'd met Phoebe Gates somewhere else. Anywhere but the house. She had a warmth about her. A glow. And an honesty about her that was sometimes missing in the people he normally came across.

But this was business. This was family business. He couldn't let it be anything else. The family had decided it was time to get rid of all reminders. And that was what Phoebe would be now, because he would forever associate her with the Hamptons house.

He dug into his pocket and pulled out a set of keys.

"Here, I got these cut for you. I'd be grateful if you could make arrangements between yourself and the caretaker to give all the trade personnel the access that they need."

She held out her hand then paused. "What about the alarm?"

Of course. He'd forgotten about that. "Give me your phone."

"What?"

She looked surprised. He smiled as he pressed the keys into her outstretched hand. "It's a digital alarm, remember? I'll put the app and the code into your phone."

She gave him a nod and fumbled in her pocket for her phone, her fingers brushing against his as she handed it over. He ignored the tingle—that little acknowledgement of warmth as skin contacted with skin. For the second time in as many minutes he reminded himself this was a business arrangement and focused on the phone.

It was more outdated than he would have expected.

Most business people he worked with had the latest version of everything. After a few seconds he frowned. "No signal. We'll need to go someplace else so I can input the code."

He paused for a second as he looked at the loaded trolley. There really was no room for anything else. "Are you done?"

She bit her lip and shook her head. "I just need to pick some leather." She counted down on her list. "There are seven sofas to be recovered, and twenty chairs."

"How many?" His brain was beginning to throb. It was clear that even though he could manage multiple dealings in his company, across different time zones and continents—the minutiae of dealing with preparing a house for sale were beyond him.

She gave a smile and arched one eyebrow. "But hey? How long does it take to buy some fabric and some vases?" There was a twinkle in her eyes that he knew he deserved.

He couldn't help but smile. In the last two days she'd literally sketched designs for every room in two color palettes, organized refitting of the kitchen and some of the bathrooms, decided what pieces to keep and which to refurbish, all without any help. He held up his hands. "Okay, you got me. I didn't really know what it was that you did."

"But you hired me for a quarter of a million dollars anyway?"

He didn't quite know how to respond to that, but Phoebe was already off again, talking to the assistant. "Is this the way to the leather?"

An hour later Matteo had seen, touched and smelt more varieties of leather than he'd ever really known existed and, even though he had no experience, it felt as if Phoebe had chosen well. She was still talking though. "I have a van parked outside. Can I get everything transferred into that?" she asked the assistant.

Matteo interrupted. "You brought a van? You're not getting everything delivered?"

She shook her head. "Why would I do that? I want to take everything back to the house myself. I want to check I'm happy with the fabrics before I get the drapes and furnishings made up. The leather will be delivered direct to the upholsterer, and tomorrow the chairs and sofas will be taken to his workshop so his team can get started."

Matteo pulled his credit card from his pocket and settled the bill. Yes, it was large. But no more than he'd really expected. The whole inside of the house needed a facelift, and he knew it.

Phoebe was still chattering away. She was very self-effacing but also extremely efficient. She had a way of getting things done. And she'd certainly moved with speed.

Something inside him was twisting around. It had to be the house. It had been so long since he'd actually been there, that it was only natural returning would be unsettling. But that didn't explain why he couldn't seem to take his eyes away from the girl in the bright pink coat, with the mad curls and coffee-tinted skin.

She bent down and talked to a toddler in a stroller while the mother was paying for her purchases, tracing her finger around the little one's palm as she sang "Ring-a-Ring o' Roses."

All of the women he'd been involved with spent their lives dressed in suits and formal dresses. Phoebe was wearing jeans, boots and a pale blue jumper under her coat. He liked her like that.

*Like.* A word he hadn't contemplated in a while. He could almost hear the roaring in his ears. When was the last time he'd actually liked someone?

He pushed the thoughts from his mind. His phone signal was still poor, and he still had to put the alarm code into Phoebe's phone. He had work to do. Being around Phoebe seemed to permanently distract him.

"Phoebe, do you want to grab some lunch? We need to find a place with a better signal so I can put the alarm code into your phone."

Phoebe looked surprised. "Well, sure. But don't you need to go back into the city? Because I was going to head down to the Hamptons."

Why was he doing this? His head wasn't entirely sure. The logical part of his brain was telling him this made perfect sense, it was all about an alarm code. If Phoebe had her own set of keys and the alarm code, then there was no reason for her to bother him again.

But even the rational part of his brain could sense this was a smoke screen. Whether he wanted to admit it, or not.

Phoebe licked her lips. They were painted pink today to match her coat, but the truth was she didn't need any makeup. Her natural beauty shone through. From the glow in her cheeks, to the shine on her springy curls and the sparkle in her eyes.

Matteo nodded. "Let's head toward the Hamptons. I'll get the driver to follow you. We can pull in at the first café we see in Westhampton."

Phoebe gave a nod. "You'll need to give me time to get the van loaded."

More time. There was only one thing for it.

He gave a nod of his head and held out his hands. "What am I here for?"

* * *

She wasn't quite sure what was going on. Matteo Bianchi was still as confusing as ever. One second he was a pleasant guy with a spark in his eye and a sense of humor, next second he was a grump, with dark shadows sweeping across his face. She wasn't sure whether he really found her a hindrance or a help.

She'd tried her best not to laugh as his suit had got wrinkled and smudged as he'd helped load up the van. She imagined that Matteo spent most of his life looking immaculate. Much like the people around him. Why did she get the feeling she'd never fit in?

Her stomach gave a growl as she arrived in Westhampton and signaled to pull into the parking lot. There were numerous cafés around and she was sure they would find something good to eat in most of them.

Matteo's driver was close behind her and by the time she'd locked up the van, Matteo was standing on the sidewalk waiting for her. He gestured toward the Rose Bakery Café, adorned with yellow cladding and with red and white awning flickering in the strong winds. "Want to try in here?"

There was a smell of cinnamon wafting from the front door. "Absolutely." She smiled.

They walked up the steps and he held the door open for her. The waitress quickly showed them to a table, gave them some menus and took their order for drinks.

Phoebe let out a laugh as her stomach gave an obligatory growl. "What do you want to eat?" Matteo asked.

Phoebe closed her eyes for a second and breathed in deeply. "There's far too many delicious smells in here. I can smell omelets, cinnamon buns, raspberry croissants and some delicious soups."

He leaned across the table toward her. It was the first

time she'd had a chance to notice the shadow along his jaw. Or the lines around his eyes. She rested her elbows on the table. It was so easy to lean forward too. "Are you okay, Matteo? Did you sleep last night?"

He blinked but didn't pull back. He just tipped his head a little to the side. "I hate that you do that sometimes."

"What?" He might be saying he hated her, but the expression on his face was telling her a whole other story.

He sighed as the waitress appeared with their drinks. "Blindside me." He stared down at his Americano and laughed. He gave his head a shake. "Not many people in this life can do that."

She licked her lips and smiled as the waitress stood poised with her order pad. "What'll it be, folks?"

Phoebe looked at the waitress with hopeful eyes. "What kind of soup do you have?"

The waitress checked her pad. "Today we have potato chowder, lentil and bacon, and chicken and rice."

"I'll have the potato chowder, please."

Matteo nodded. "I'll have the omelet, please, with mushrooms and cheese."

The waitress raised her eyebrows. "With salad or fries?"

"Salad, thanks." The waitress gave a nod and waved her hand at the glass cabinet behind her. "Just remember, we have some great desserts too."

Phoebe watched her saunter away then smiled at Matteo. "Do you think our order wasn't big enough for her?"

He shrugged. "Hey, she's right. They do have some great desserts. Maybe we'll have some pie."

Phoebe leaned her head on one hand as she stirred

her caramel latte. "You don't strike me as a pie kind of guy."

He raised his eyebrows. "I don't? What kind of guy do I strike you as?"

She kept stirring her coffee as she contemplated her answer. "I think you might be a bit of a traditionalist. I'm surprised you didn't try and steer us toward an Italian restaurant instead of a bakery."

He gave a slow nod of his head. "Any other insights you want to share about me?"

This time his voice had the slightest edge. As if he were silently putting up walls between them.

She couldn't help herself. She just started speaking. "You haven't shaved. Last time I saw you, you were immaculate. And you look tired today. I'm sorry if I offended you. Because I didn't mean to. I was just worried about you, because you looked so tired. You offered to help load the van and came out of your way to have lunch with me."

"Do you always worry about people you hardly know?"

His steady green eyes were fixed on hers. She held her breath. She should take it as a compliment, but he hadn't quite phrased it that way. He'd phrased it more as if she were just far too nosey.

She remembered talking to Captain Monaghan in the hospital. He'd been exhausted—and very sick. When she'd gone to get some light refreshments for her mother, she'd offered to get some for Rudy too. In fact, she'd ended up getting food and drinks for most of the other patients. It was her nature. Her way. She couldn't and wouldn't change it because Matteo Bianchi found her intrusive.

She shrugged and smiled. "Some people say I have a kind heart. I can live with that."

As she looked up Matteo was studying her hard. A frown creased his brow and he leaned closer and lifted his fingers to her cheek. The contact made her flinch.

"Phoebe, did someone hurt you? Is that a bruise?"

She shook her head as she lifted her own hand to her cheek. "Don't panic. It's me." She lowered her gaze, almost embarrassed to answer. "In my excitement to get started this morning I fell out of bed. I hit my face on my bedside cabinet."

Matteo didn't speak. He just kept staring. Then he glanced down at her hand. She could see the tension across his shoulders and the tic at the side of his jaw. "Is there someone in your life, Phoebe?"

She jerked and sat back in her seat, her mouth instantly dry. Everything about this felt wrong. He'd more or less just accused her of being too nosey, but now she could feel the intensity of his gaze. She could see both the sympathy and revulsion in his eyes. He'd jumped to a conclusion that was entirely wrong. She didn't doubt for a second what Matteo Bianchi would do to a man who was abusing his wife.

Tears pooled in her eyes. But for none of the reasons that Matteo was obviously assuming. She opened her mouth to speak but the words stuck in her throat. Why were they so hard to say?

"There…there's…no one in my life, just me." She shook her head as the tears threatened to fall. "Can't blame anyone else for my clumsiness."

His shoulders fell a little but the crease in his brow remained.

The waitress appeared at that second, gave them a

peculiar glance and put their plates on the table. "Anything else?"

Phoebe shook her head quickly. "We're fine," replied Matteo.

They sat in silence for a few seconds. Phoebe staring at her potato chowder. The smell that had seemed so delicious earlier, now just seemed to make her stomach do uncomfortable flip-flops.

Matteo lifted his fork and picked at his omelet. After a few seconds he let out a sigh and put his fork back down, sliding his hand over the table and letting it cover hers.

"Is there anything you need to tell me?"

She shook her head as one tear finally slid down her cheek. The lump in her throat had grown to epic proportions. Her other hand was still automatically stirring her soup.

Matteo pressed his lips together for a moment. His hand was warm against hers. Her fingers had never felt quite so cold. Up until a few moments ago she'd felt fine. Now, she just felt so...empty.

Why? Jason had died three years ago. She'd had to tell friends and family about the terrible accident. But she'd simply never found herself in a circumstance like this.

Matteo was only showing concern over something he'd misinterpreted. It should be no big deal. She should just have waved her hand and laughed it off.

But when he'd stared at her with those big green eyes and asked her if there was someone in her life it was the first time in three years she actually felt *something*.

And that terrified her.

She shook her head and stared down at her soup. She could tell him why she was tearful. She could tell him that her fiancé had died a few years before. Then, he would know that there was no hint of trouble in her life.

But somehow she couldn't find the words.

She'd tried dating. Once or twice. But her heart just wasn't in it. Jason had held every part of her heart. She'd loved him. Totally. He'd been her soul mate. And when he'd died? She'd tried so hard to soldier on.

But the hurt was inexplicable. Something she could never, ever forget. And it had made her learn to build walls, put up barriers, to keep herself safe. It was the only way. She couldn't—*wouldn't*—ever allow herself to feel like that again.

Which was why being around Matteo and feeling something again—no matter how small and unexplained—was unsettling her beyond words.

But then he did something unexpected. His hand was already sitting over hers. He gave it a squeeze and gestured down to their plates. "I think maybe our waitress was right. I think we should move straight on to desserts. Why waste time when we both know we want an explosion of sweetness?" He stood up and took her hand in his, pulling her up toward him and giving the waitress a wave. Phoebe's legs were shaking. What on earth was wrong with her?

But Matteo did his best to put her at ease by throwing a relaxed arm behind her waist and moving her a little closer to the glass counter. The waitress gestured toward the cakes. "What'll it be?"

Matteo nudged Phoebe. "What's your favorite?"

There was a mountain of choice. Chocolate cake, cheesecake, carrot cake, apple pie, cherry pie, strawberry shortcake, cupcakes and cookies. Too much choice. She couldn't even pick. Matteo waved his hand. "Just give us one of everything. We'll share."

The words seem to bring her back to her senses. "Matteo? We'll never be able to eat all that."

He smiled. "No. But we can take a bite of each. Can't you remember as a kid always wanting to do something like that? Let's relive a bit of our childhoods."

It was the most relaxed she'd seen him. They sat back down at their table and the waitress brought over a large tray with every dessert on a separate plate and lots of cutlery. She topped up their drinks, cleared away their other plates, then left them to it.

Phoebe picked up her fork as Matteo raised his eyebrows. "How do you want to do this? A bite each?"

Phoebe put her fork against her lips. "That sounds fair. But who gets to go first?"

He smiled. "Well, that's easy. My grandmother trained me well. Ladies first."

Phoebe took a deep breath. The tension was finally starting to leave her muscles. She grinned and reached over, digging her fork into the carrot cake with frosting. It was delicious.

She took a sip of her coffee and sat back in the seat. Matteo grinned back and didn't hesitate, heading straight for the cherry pie. "You thought I wasn't really a pie kind of guy? Well, watch and learn. Apple, peach, plum, cherry, I'm not fussy. I'll take them all."

"Does anyone else get to try the cherry pie?" She snagged a little from the side. "Hmm. Lovely."

She gave another smile. "So, I take it the sugar burst is helping with the tiredness?"

His eyes widened in surprise. He'd just gotten a forkful of chocolate cake. He stared at it for a second then nodded. "Actually it is. Do I really look that bad?"

She shook her head. "Of course not. Just tired. Were

you working late? I imagine it's hard coordinating things on different continents."

He pressed his lips together for a second. "Sometimes." He lowered his eyes as he ate the piece of chocolate cake.

Phoebe tried the strawberry shortcake. "Oh, wow, this is delicious. It's my favorite."

Matteo looked up. "Why don't you just finish it? Go on."

She shook her head and put her fork down. "No, honestly, I couldn't. But—you were right—just being able to take a bite out of each is fabulous." She put both hands on the table. "Thank you for this, Matteo. I'm so looking forward to getting this job started. The house is just wonderful. And I promise, once I'm sure about the fabrics, I'll get the order for the drapes placed. The painters start tomorrow and I've already agreed on the colors for every room. The only other major thing I need to see about is replacing some of the carpets." She was starting to babble again. She couldn't help it. Interior design was the area she was comfortable with. She couldn't wait to get started on the job.

But instead of being enthused by her response it was almost as if Matteo switched off. The warmth that had been in his eyes seemed to dissipate.

She kept talking. "Do you want to look at some more of my sketches? Is there anything you'd like to discuss about them? I am open to any changes."

Matteo shook his head and held out his hand. "Give me your phone and I'll put the alarm code in for you."

She handed the phone over and he programmed it in a few seconds.

His phone buzzed and he stood up. "Like I said, I'm happy for you to carry on with the changes. You've told me about most of them, and I've seen some of the sketches. That's enough. I don't need to know the details. I'll contact the bank and make sure your card is activated. You can let me know when you're done. At that point, we can discuss the house in Rome."

She could almost feel all the blood being sucked from her body. Rome. A few plane rides away. They hadn't really mentioned it.

She'd had a chance. She'd had a chance to tell Matteo the truth about her life, and the fact a plane ride might not be so easy for her.

But when the chance had arisen, she just couldn't find the words. Pathetic really.

It wasn't as if it were a state secret. But saying the words herself was different.

And saying the words to a man she barely knew, who was confusing her in a dozen different ways, wasn't exactly easy.

She took back her phone when he offered it and turned it over in her hand. It looked easy enough. She just had to bring up the barcode and show it to the reader on the alarm.

"This will be fine, thanks."

Matteo nodded and picked up the check. The sparkle from his eyes had vanished. The façade was back in place. What was it with this man?

She watched as he settled the check and then headed to the door. He paused, as if his manners were telling him he should wait for her, but she shook her head. "Go ahead." She glanced down at the table. "I'm going to pack some of these up. The tradesmen that are coming to do some of the jobs will be grateful."

She lifted her chin as she tried to calm her jangling nerves.

It was amazing. One minute he was cold and distant, the next, care and compassion seemed to shine from those dark eyes. But nothing seemed to meet in the middle. She felt like Belle in *Beauty and the Beast*, torn between two people.

If this was how it was going to be, how on earth would she survive the next four weeks?

# CHAPTER FOUR

THREE DAYS. THAT was how long she'd been here. Phoebe always worked long hours on the job once she got started and this house was no different.

With the avocado bathroom gone, the walls were now smooth and ready for retiling. The plumbing and electrics had been checked and any problems fixed. The ancient chimneys had been swept. The whole house smelled of paint, and there was a perpetual thin layer of dust wherever she went.

It wasn't that the clean-up crew weren't doing their job. They were. It was just they were having to do their job over and over again as the endless stream of tradesmen came and went from the house.

Today there was a joiner oiling and re-hanging some of the shutters. They really were gorgeous and they'd all been repainted a brilliant white. The kitchen appliances had been delivered, but not connected. The Belfast sinks were still to be fitted along with the new countertop. Phoebe had a spreadsheet with all times, dates and phone numbers for everyone responsible.

She walked up the curved stairs humming to herself with a pile of bedding and towels in her arms. Two of the bedrooms and half-baths were ready for her inspection. The drapes for the bedrooms wouldn't be here for another week. But there was no reason she couldn't start to look at some of the finishing touches.

The porcelain sink and toilet gleamed bright white, along with the tiles. The clean-up crew had guaranteed they could restore the pieces to their former glory and they'd been as good as their word. She smiled as she put the pale yellow towels on the floor. She'd bought some cute ottomans for the bathrooms. She'd need to find them.

She glanced out the window toward Lake Mecox. Snow was starting to fall heavily again. She had hours of work still to do. She didn't want to start the journey back home because of the bad weather—even more so, she didn't want any of the tradesmen to leave early.

She'd ordered new mattresses for all the beds. So she spent a few minutes making up the bed in one set of bedclothes, then five minutes later in another. The pale yellow had seemed a little washed out in this room. The duck-egg blue was much better. Most people didn't understand how much light played in dressing a house. One of the first things she considered was whether a room was south, east, north or west facing. It could make all the difference.

She looked at the pile of bedclothes she still had to go through. There was no reason why she couldn't start looking at the other rooms. She had cushions, new lights, new lamp shades. There was a world of work she could do right now. Enthusiasm sparked inside her. Now, where had she put those prints she'd bought the other day?

"You look like crap."

Brianna had never been one to hold back.

Matteo waved his hand and shook his head while he

finished his call. Brianna swept through the door and strode across his office. She was wearing a bright blue designer coat that she took off and practically dumped in his lap.

Patience had never been his sister's greatest virtue.

She sighed, then tapped the desk, before finally perching on the edge of it. Matteo finished his call then leant back in his chair. "What do you want?"

He knew not to ignore her. Any man who ignored Brianna Bianchi was a fool, and soon learned the consequences of their actions.

"I'm ready to meet her."

"Ready to meet who?"

She waved her hand nonchalantly. "That girl that you won't really talk about. Makes me suspicious. I definitely have to meet her."

Matteo shook his head as he stared at the laptop on his desk. There was a problem at one of the vineyards in Portugal. He really needed to call. Soon.

Brianna licked her glossy lips. As usual, his sister looked impeccable. And very much like their mother.

Brianna always liked to be reminded of that. She'd only been a few weeks old when their mother had died, so didn't have any memories of her at all—only a few family photographs. But for Matteo it was harder. He had lots of memories.

Brianna had the same shiny dark hair and eyes, the same skin tone and frame. It was uncanny, and sometimes she even did little movements similar to their mother. There was no way it could be learned behavior. It could only be genetics. And sometimes that terrified Matteo. Especially now.

He'd always been close to his brother and sister. How would they feel about him if he ever told them the truth about their mother? Would they hate him, resent him for keeping quiet? He couldn't bear the thought of not being this close to them. His insides twisted again. For now, it was best that he continued to keep his secret. He could watch Brianna. Keep close to her. That way, he'd know if there was anything to worry about. He wasn't a child anymore. He was an adult. An informed adult.

Brianna rested her hands on her swollen abdomen. "What's she like anyway? I looked her up. She's pretty." She gave Matteo a sideways glance. "Very pretty, actually. And she wasn't wearing a ring in the picture that I found. Is she attached?"

Matteo couldn't even hide his surprise at his sister's brazenness. "Why on earth would that matter?"

Brianna arched her back then stood up and walked around the desk, all the while her eyes carefully focused on her brother. "Well, of course, it doesn't. I'm just curious. How soon will she be finished?"

Matteo kept his voice steady. "Just a few weeks, I expect. Phoebe seems super-organized. She's running the place like an army colonel."

Brianna's eyes gleamed and she leaned across the desk toward him. "So, it's Phoebe already, and not Ms. Gates?"

He met her gaze square on. "Stop it, Brianna. You being pregnant won't prevent me from throwing you out of my office."

She threw back her head and laughed. "As if." Then her face fell a little. "I'm twitchy. I feel as if I'm going stir crazy. I'd love to be at the house in Rome. I'd love to help with the renovations." She rested her hands on her stomach. "But *some people* have decided I shouldn't fly."

He couldn't help but smile. "The whole world thinks you shouldn't fly right now."

Brianna bit her bottom lip and gave him *that* look. The one she always used when she wanted something.

"What? What is it?"

"I wondered if you would mind having a look for something for me."

Matteo frowned. "What do you mean?"

Brianna averted her gaze. "I've been looking for some photographs. Dad told me about them. But he could never find them."

Matteo felt a chill across his skin. "What photographs?"

Brianna licked her lips. He could tell she'd been practicing this conversation in her head. "Their wedding photographs. Dad thought he might have left them in the house. He said that they might have been left in one of the cupboards. They're in a red photograph album."

Matteo could feel every little hair on the back of his neck stand on end. "Dad told you this when?"

Brianna lifted her darkened eyelids. "Just before he died. He told me he wanted me to see their wedding pictures. So I would always remember just how happy they'd been." Her voice shook a little. And that for Brianna was big. She hardly ever let her emotions betray her. "It was just after I told him I was pregnant."

"And you just mention this now?" Brianna flinched at his snappiness.

He cringed. He couldn't help it.

Brianna waved her hand angrily. "There's never been a good time. Dad was sick, then he died. Then we had to sort out the business. Then it was Christmas and we had to agree about the house sales. Now *is* the time to talk about this. Before we sell the house at the Hamptons."

She blew part of her fringe off her face. "If this is such a bother for you, Matteo, I'll do it myself. I thought, since you'd already spent some time down there, it might be something you could do." She lifted her chin and stared off into the corner. "I could always ask Vittore."

She knew just what buttons to press. Always had. Always would. The gift of being a sister.

"Which cupboard? Where?"

She shrugged. "He wasn't specific. He just said that they'd cleared things out quickly and maybe the photographs had been left behind."

Matteo sucked in a deep breath in an effort to keep calm. He didn't want Brianna to know how difficult he was finding this. He didn't want to give any indication of how many memories being back at the house had stirred up. He was head of the family now. He had to show strength. Resilience. And he had that in spades. It just felt as if he'd had to keep reminding himself of that in the last few days.

His eyes rested on his sister's stomach. Especially now. How could he say no? He stood up quickly. "Of course I'll look for the album. If it's there—I'll find it."

He walked across the room and dropped a kiss on her cheek. "I'll let you know how I get on."

Brianna gave a nod of her head. "I knew I could count on you."


"Phoebe? Do you realize what time it is?"

Phoebe jerked up from where she'd been contemplating how to redress the gorgeous library. She'd missed this room on her first visit to the house. It seemed that when the Bianchis had first moved in they hadn't gotten around to clearing out the masses of books that the former actress had owned. Some of the subject matter almost made Phoebe blush. It seemed there had been much more to the demure actress than met the eye.

She turned to the door where Al, one of the joiners, was standing. His tool chest was in his hand and he was already wearing his jacket. She looked at her watch.

"Seven o'clock? Really? I had no idea. Al, I'm sorry. It's New Year's Eve. You should have gone home an hour ago."

Al shrugged. "I was in the middle of things, but I'm going to head off now. Family party. The snow is getting worse. Where do you live? I'm in Hoboken. Can I drop you somewhere?"

Phoebe shook her head swiftly. "No, of course not. I'm fine. I have my car."

Al raised his eyebrows. "Be careful out there. I'm not sure your car is designed for roads covered in snow. And it already looks as if some of the New Year revelers are out."

She gave a smile and nodded. "No problems."

Al disappeared and thirty minutes later Phoebe had finally decided on a plan for the library. She'd never been a fan of New Years. Her mom had let her know well in advance that she was having a glass of wine with a neighbor, then going home to bed. Phoebe had no reason to rush back into the city and experience the Times Square madness. She walked through to the kitchen with her sketch pad in her hands. The window ledge of the kitchen was stacked with snow. Phoebe wrinkled her brow and sat the pad down on the large kitchen table. Maybe she *should* head home—that snow was deeper than she'd expected.

She grabbed her bag and jacket and headed to the front door. The sky was already black and the snow was swirling around. Her Mini was coated in a thick layer of it. She smiled. Most New Yorkers saw no need for a car. Transport in the city was good. But Phoebe's interior design job meant she frequently needed to travel further afield.

She'd watched a movie years ago that featured three of these cars and had dreamed of one ever since. When she'd found a second-hand one—that came from the UK—a few months ago, she'd had to buy it.

The driveway was thick with ice and Phoebe practically skidded as she headed to the car. She jumped inside and started the engine. The car was always reliable and turned over first time. But as she moved the car into first gear—she'd finally got used to the stick shift—the wheels spun in the snow. She tried again, and again, but the car didn't move.

Somewhere in the distance fireworks exploded in the dark sky. It seemed that the Hampton parties had started already. People weren't waiting for the stroke of midnight for the fun to start. She could only imagine the chaos around Times Square right now with people crushing in, waiting to see the famous ball drop. Did she really want to head back there?

She sighed and leaned back in her seat as the thick flakes of snow continued to fall. She stared back at the house. Just as well she loved the place—looked as if she'd have to stay.

Phoebe scrambled back out of the car and into the house. Now the work crew had all left it was amazing how much her footsteps echoed through the house. She pulled out her phone and searched for the nearest pizza place—thank goodness it was still open. Two minutes later she'd ordered, warning their delivery driver about the driveway.

She glanced at her phone and sent a quick text to

her mother. It would be so easy to sit down and spend all night on social media, but it wasn't really what she wanted to do. None of the TVs in the house was currently working. The satellite company wasn't scheduled to arrive until next week.

She smiled. Of course. The library. The perfect place to spend a snow-filled evening. It was stacked with multiple shelves of books, accessible by an old-style set of moving steps. In a way, it was the perfect place for her to see in the New Year.

She grabbed the bag she carried with her. Unlike some interior designers she always had a change of clothes so she could do as much physical work as possible. It only took ten minutes to head upstairs and shower and change into the gray sweatpants and long-sleeved pink top she had with her. Comfort first. The bed that she'd made up earlier looked good. Only thing was, the room was a little cold. The heating system was something she'd have to look at the next day. It might be a bit chilly, but staying here wouldn't be such a hardship.

She headed back down the stairs and spent fifteen minutes trying to light the fire in the library. Eventually she conceded defeat and did an Internet search and watched a video that showed her how to do it. Five minutes later she finally had the flicker of flames, followed by the arrival of her pizza. The delivery guy gave her a wry smile. "Just as well we have a four-by-four. Your driveway doesn't take any prisoners. And I'm heading home now."

Phoebe nodded and smiled as she paid him and gave him a big tip. "Thanks so much for this. Happy New Year. Drive safely."

*Your driveway.* The guy was assuming she actually owned the house. Maybe in some wild dream or fantasy she would actually own a house in the Hamptons. Phoebe couldn't stop smiling as she closed the door.

The pizza was lukewarm. But it didn't matter. She hadn't realized she was quite so hungry. She carried it through to the library and looked around. Even though the fire was lit she still felt a little cold. She hesitated for only a few seconds before she ran back up the stairs and pulled the new bedclothes from the bed. There was no point in being cold.

Two slices of pizza later, she'd found a book that could make her hair curl even tighter and she settled down on the rug in front of the fire. This could be interesting.

Matteo let out another curse as his car skidded and he struggled to stop the back end fishtailing. Although the roads from the city had been glistening with snow, the gritters had been out and main highways were clear. The roads through the hamlets and villages of the Hamptons were a little different. He'd had the choice of any car in the garage and had chosen the one he'd thought most practical. The large four-by-four had initially made the journey easy, but the hardest part of the journey was now his own driveway. It currently resembled some kind of ice rink.

He frowned as he finally pulled up outside the house. He'd never intended to be this late, but a conference call had gone on much longer than expected. So by the time he'd started the journey to the Hamptons it was already dark. There was another car sitting in front of the house—one he didn't recognize.

It was New Year's Eve. Who on earth would still be here? Chances were it was nobody. Maybe one of the workers had decided to take a ride home with someone else—perhaps to join in some New Year's celebrations.

Matteo had tactfully given apologies to three potential party invitations, and the last place on earth he wanted to be right now was in the heart of New York at Times Square. The streets had been crammed as he'd left the city and they'd be worse by now.

He stepped outside of the car and promptly landed on his butt. He got up quicker than he'd gone down, groaning and rubbing his backside, flicking his head from side to side. Of course no one had seen him—no one was here. But his reactions were just automatic. He pulled his phone from his pocket praying the screen wasn't smashed.

The spider's web across the glass told him otherwise.

He held it up to the alarm scanner. Nothing. Nothing happened. He tried again, then frowned as he turned the key in the lock. A couple of seconds and a few careful steps later he was inside the house.

As soon as he was in the entrance hall he knew something wasn't right.

There was…something.

A noise. A smell.

He turned in that direction and started walking. At the end of the corridor there was a glow. None of the lights were on in this part of the house. He could easily flick the switches. But he was far too stubborn minded to slow down. He shook his head as he kept walking. For the first time since he'd been a teenager, every bad horror movie he'd ever watched suddenly made sense. He'd always shouted at the screen before—*why haven't you put on the lights? Why are you walking toward the trouble?* But here he was, doing exactly the same.

That car still bothered him. But it could easily belong

to one of the clean-up crew who didn't want to drive a small car home in the snow and had traveled home with someone else. The door had been locked, but the alarm hadn't been on.

Could this be an intruder? Someone who'd heard the house was being renovated and had decided there might be something worth stealing?

His hands clenched into fists. Matteo didn't need any kind of weapon. He was more than a match for any intruder.

As he strode down the corridor he realized where the light was coming from. The library? Why on earth would any intruder go to the library? It was a place he'd never spent much time in; he hadn't even remembered to direct Phoebe here when she was looking around the house.

There was something strange about the light. And the smell. Was something burning?

His heart rate quickened as he swung the door open—to the most peaceful scene.

Phoebe was lying curled up on the floor, covered in blankets in front of a flickering fire.

A fire. Of course. Although the house had multiple fireplaces, Matteo had never seen any of the fires lit in this house. They'd only stayed here for a few weeks one fateful summer. It hadn't even occurred to him that the light might be coming from one of the fireplaces.

Phoebe's curls were fanned out all around her, her head on a cushion that must have come from one of the high-back chairs. On the floor in front of her was a pizza box, with only a few slices missing.

For a few moments he didn't move. Just watched the rise and fall of her chest. Her skin glowed in the orange flickering flames. Her lips full and pink.

Something clenched inside him and he turned away. She was an employee. A business associate. Even if it was for only a few weeks. He had to push any other kind of thoughts away. He had too much else to deal with—too much else to worry about. He couldn't afford any distractions.

"Matteo?"

He turned around. Phoebe was pushing herself up, moving her hair away from her tired eyes. "When did you get here?" She looked confused. "What time is it?"

Matteo straightened up. "It's after ten. Phoebe, what are you doing here? It's New Year's Eve. Are you staying here?"

She gave a weak smile. "I kind of got snowed in. My Mini wouldn't move. The wheels just kept spinning in the snow. They couldn't get any grip."

She looked down at the bedding around her, and pulled a face as if she realized how inappropriate it might look. "I'm sorry about this. I came down here because I was cold. We'll need to check the boilers. Once I'd lit the fire and had something to eat, I just closed my eyes for a second and…" Her voice tailed off, then she let out a little laugh and pulled her knees up to her chest. "But isn't this the perfect place to spend New Year's?"

The heat from the room reached out toward Matteo. The fire was inviting. But the sleepy-eyed woman seemed even more so. It was the expression on her face when she said those words. Any other woman that Matteo had been involved with would have made a song and dance about New Year's Eve and parties. More than once he'd ended up spending New Year's dressed in a tuxedo and celebrating with people he barely knew, as the woman on his arm complained about her shoes and drank more champagne. He wasn't at all sorry not to be in that situation this year.

Phoebe, in her casual clothes, with pizza and a bed in front of the fire, was like a revelation.

He stepped inside. Phoebe gave a rueful smile and held up the pizza box. "Can I offer you some cold pizza? The delivery guy managed to get here, so pizza—" she looked around "—and soda is all I can offer you."

Matteo shook his head. "I didn't come here for food."

"Oh, what did you come for?"

The question was innocent. He knew that. But it sent up all his defenses. "Just something for the family."

Phoebe looked at him curiously as she pushed herself to her feet. "Can I help you?"

She moved over toward him, obviously feeling self-conscious as she tugged at her clothes. "Not the most professional-looking—I know. But, sometimes dressing homes isn't as glamorous as it sounds. Sometimes I just get down on my hands and knees and scrub floors."

Something flared in his mind. A few years ago he'd sold another property. The interior designer hired then had swanned around in a suit and heels with her hair swept up in a bun, a scarf around her neck and a clipboard permanently in her hand. Ms. Dragon, as he'd nicknamed her, wouldn't ever dream of getting her hands dirty. She was too busy ordering her minions about. There was something reassuring about knowing how committed to the job Phoebe was.

Phoebe tilted her head to the side and a waft of roses seemed to reach out toward him. It took him a few seconds to realize the scent was coming from her. Had she just showered? "It's late. Couldn't what you need wait until morning?" Phoebe turned and walked to the window, pulling back the shutters and looking at the white landscape outside. "If you're not careful, you'll end up just as stranded as me."

Matteo walked up behind her, standing a little closer than he should. The scent of roses was definitely coming from her. Fresh and light, it was almost intoxicating. Maybe it was the heat from the fire? Or maybe it was just his lack of sleep catching up with him. But something was sending all his senses into overload.

"What brought you to the library?" Matteo looked around the room. It was darker than the rest of the house, mainly because of the polished mahogany lining the shelves and walls. The only splash of color came from the wingback chairs covered in deep red velvet and the thick red rug in front of the fire. The shelves were lined with a myriad hardback books in a variety of shades that Matteo had never even looked at.

Phoebe held up her hands, her eyes sparkling. "It's the most beautiful room in the house. I love it." She walked over to the old-style moving steps. "Have you any idea how excited I was when I saw these? It's like every bookworm's dream. All these books. And these stairs? I could spend all day, every day in this room." She held up her hands in front of her chest. "I mean, imagine having a library in your house?" Her enthusiasm practically emanated from every pore.

Matteo leaned back against the wall. He'd never really thought about the library at all. He hadn't had any interest in it as a five-year-old—he'd been much more excited by the tennis court and swimming pool in the grounds of the house. But the enthusiasm brimming from Phoebe was almost infectious. He walked over and ran his hand across the spines of some of the books. The library had that old-world sort of smell. The kind you either loved—or hated.

Most of the books looked like encyclopedia-style volumes. He gave a smile. "Remember the world before the Internet, when you actually had to go to a library and search in a book when you wanted to find out something?"

Phoebe nodded. She was staring at the books in front of her. "Two seconds, that's how long it takes now to search for something. Think of the hours you had to spend before."

She was still smiling as she pulled one of the books from the shelf. "Some of these books look demure. But looks can be deceiving." There was a glint in her eye as she let the book fall open in her hands.

Matteo was curious and walked toward her. The heat in the room was building and he shrugged off his jacket. His eyes widened as he looked at the illustrations in the book and choked with laughter. He leaned closer and frowned. "Can people even get in that position?"

Phoebe met his gaze with a glint in her eye. "Only if you're a contortionist. I'm assuming these books belonged to the previous owner?"

Matteo nodded his head. He couldn't help but smile. "Melinda Mulrooney had a reputation for being demure. Seems like there was much more to her than met the eye."

Phoebe smiled as she closed the book and slid it back into place. She turned back toward Matteo and bit her lip. "I'm sorry that I'm here. Obviously, I didn't mean to be."

Matteo shrugged. "It's fine." He glanced at the heap of bedclothes on the floor. "But don't you want to sleep in a bed?"

"I would have—but it was a little cold upstairs. And what with the fire down here and—" she held out her hands "—all these wonderful books. I kind of decided that this was all the entertainment a girl could need."

The sentence was light-hearted but their gazes connected as she said the last few words. It seemed to hang in the air between them. Against the crackle of the fire in the background he could almost hear the sizzle in the air. His skin buzzed and blood rushed to parts at the rate of a Grand Prix driver racing around Le Mans. He was holding his breath without even realizing it, and as Phoebe's tongue slipped from her mouth and slid along her bottom lip it glistened in the dim light. There was a roaring in his ears. What on earth was happening between them? After the longest pause, Phoebe pulled her eyes away from his. It was excruciating.

"I've made up a few of the rooms. If you need to stay too—it should be comfortable." She pulled a face. "It just might not be too warm."

Matteo looked out of the window, trying not to let his brain go to the place it wanted to right now. Stay here? With Phoebe? The snow was falling even heavier now. The very last thing he wanted was to be stranded in this house. It didn't matter that this room was warm and inviting. It didn't matter that the house was solid, that there was food and there were beds. It was this place. For him, the heat level was irrelevant; he would always feel a chill just being here.

Phoebe reached up and touched his arm. Her warm fingertips sent a jolt through him. "Hey, you came to find something. Want some help?"

"No."

The word came out before he had time to think and Phoebe jerked backwards.

"Sorry," he said quickly as he ran his hand through his hair. He was being ridiculous. Even he knew that.

He was looking for an album he'd never seen, in a house with dozens of rooms and a million cupboards. It would be like looking for a needle in a haystack. And help should be gratefully received.

His stomach growled loudly. Phoebe pressed her lips together. "Unless you went grocery shopping, it's cold pizza, or cold pizza."

He nodded and sighed. "I guess it's cold pizza, then." He walked over and sat down on the rug in front of the fire. The snow had started to pile against the window. His stomach gave a flip as he realized there was no way he was getting out of here.

He looked down at the pizza. "What is this?"

Phoebe gave him a challenging look. "It's a mega meat feast with spicy hot sauce." She raised her eyebrows. "Why did you think I needed the soda?"

He nodded and licked his lips. "Okay then. I took you for a Hawaiian kind of girl."

"Ouch. Hawaiian is for wimps."

Matteo took a bite of the pizza. Within a few seconds the hot sauce hit his taste buds and his eyes started to water. "Wow." It came out kind of high pitched and he followed it with a deep, hearty laugh and a cough.

Phoebe laughed too and slapped his back. "Too much for you?"

He met her gaze straight on. "Not a chance." He eyed the pizza again. "I can do this. Hot sauce is nothing. I eat this kind of thing for breakfast."

"Well, don't eat it all," said Phoebe quickly. "We'll need to have it for breakfast too."

He hadn't even said the words out loud, but clearly she knew there was no way he was getting out of here tonight. Trying to travel in that thick snow would be stupid. And it was New Year's. Last thing he wanted to do was get stranded somewhere and have to call on any emergency services. Traveling now would be stupid and selfish. Matteo was neither.

He held his hand out for the soda that Phoebe passed with a laugh. "Should I have got you Hawaiian?"

He shook his head as the soda finally cooled the explosions in his taste buds.

Phoebe had pulled her knees up in front of her and leaned her head on her elbow. "So, it might be a little late, but I'm not that tired. You might not know this, but the TVs aren't working yet, and the wi-fi doesn't get fitted until next week. So, it's books or nothing."

Matteo leaned back on his hands and stretched his legs out in front of him. He might have taken his jacket off, but he was still wearing the suit he'd been dressed in all day. After sixteen hours his handmade leather shoes were starting to pinch. Phoebe looked much more comfortable than he did. "I'd kill for those sweatpants," he murmured.

Phoebe nodded and pulled at the stretchy material. "There's a reason I always have fall-back clothes." She held up her hands. "And this, is it."

Matteo shook his head. "How often do you get stranded or snowed in at work?"

Phoebe grinned. "You'd be surprised. Quite often I'm working at a place that is a bit out of the way. Or, is in the midst of renovations that means the water is turned off, or the electricity." She lifted her hands higher. "So, this is really a palace in comparison to some of the other places."

Phoebe was just so easy to be around. She was relaxed—comfortable in her own skin, and much more beautiful than she clearly realized.

But it was her manner that came over most. She had

a good heart. Five minutes in her company virtually told you everything you'd ever need to know. She'd never be the person who was thoughtless or insincere. Business had made him hard. He was used to ruthlessness and backstabbing. It was refreshing to be in different company.

The only light in the room was the flickering flames and right now they were reflecting off Phoebe's dark brown eyes. The noise from the fire—and the occasional spark—was actually very peaceful. For a few seconds he was sorely tempted just to sit here.

But Phoebe had already said she wasn't tired—clearly, because she'd already slept. But how to spend the next few hours?

He took a deep breath. He only had one reason for being here. And the truth was, he didn't even know where to start looking. Would it really be so hard for him to actually ask for a little help? He met Phoebe's gaze again. "How about we play a game of hide and seek?"

She gave herself a shake. Had she just heard him correctly? It was possible she was hallucinating. In fact, it was possible she'd gone back to that dream state she'd thought she was in last week when she'd first met Italian stallion, Matteo Bianchi.

She tried not to smile at the nickname her brain had automatically conjured up for him.

Chances were, she was still sleeping in front of that crackling fire after getting snowed in. Matteo Bianchi wasn't really sitting by her side, with his shirtsleeves pushed up and his dark hair flopping over his mesmerizing eyes. That would just be too good to be true. Really.

His hand closed over hers. Warmth. Heat. "What do you say?"

Nope. She wasn't sleeping. She was definitely awake. A dream wouldn't be making her heart beat so fast she couldn't breathe.

"Hide and seek?" Her brain couldn't really compute. He wanted to play a childhood game with her?

He nodded and changed position so he was kneeling next to her. "I told you that I came here to find something. Truth is, I'm not even sure where to look."

She frowned. "What do you mean?"

His voice was steady. "I'm looking for an old photo album. There's no guarantee it's even here, but my family think it could be in a cupboard somewhere."

The frown on her forehead deepened. Her head flicked from side to side. "In a cupboard, in here?"

In a place this size, how would they ever find it?

But Phoebe managed to shake off the enormity of the task quickly. Matteo had come all this way on New Year's Eve to find a family heirloom. The least she could do was be helpful. "Any clues? Do you know any more about it?"

He hesitated. "I know it's red. And it's their wedding album."

"Whose wedding album?"

He sucked in a deep breath. "My parents'."

"They lost their wedding album?" She didn't mean for it to come out like that—as if she almost couldn't believe someone would lose something so precious.

She watched him swallow as he waved his hand. "There was a lot going on the last time we were here. My mother was—ill. My father just recently died and my sister would really like to find the album."

There it was again. That little feeling she sometimes got around Matteo. He was telling her something—but not everything. Not that it was any of her business. She had no right to pry and ask questions. But she couldn't pretend she wasn't curious.

She pushed herself up onto her knees, mirroring his position. "Okay, so we're looking for a red wedding album somewhere in this house. Do you have any idea at all where it might be?"

He shook his head. Phoebe put her hand on her chin and thought hard. "Okay, so I've been in some of the cupboards in the bedrooms and bathrooms—and I've definitely been in every one of the kitchen cupboards, and each of them were empty. There might have been some old cleaning products, or dishcloths, but I haven't found anything personal at all. In fact—" she leaned a bit and looked around the room "—this place, these books, are the most personal things that I've found. But these didn't belong to your family."

Matteo's face fell a little. "Maybe this is all a wild goose chase."

She hated that. She hated seeing him look defeated. She grabbed his hand. "Get up. Let's think about this." Matteo stood next to her, as she started to walk around. She smiled at him and followed his example from earlier. "Let's play hide and seek. So, we don't think it's deliberately hidden somewhere?"

He shook his head.

"Okay, then, if you'd just moved in somewhere new—" she glanced at Matteo again "—and you had young kids—and you had plans to pretty much renovate the whole house—where would you put something precious? Where would someplace safe be?"

Matteo looked around too, as if he were trying to follow her train of thought. He gave her a hopeful smile. "Let's find out."

Almost two hours later they sagged back into the library. Even though the clean-up crew had been through the entire house more than once, it turned out that poking around the back of cupboards could still leave your hair and clothes covered in dust.

He was tired. He was definitely cranky. And even the woman who'd already had some sleep seemed to be flagging. He was ready to give up. The snow was still thick and heavy outside and it looked as if the gritters hadn't made it onto the roads yet. He'd definitely be spending the rest of the night here.

Phoebe flopped down for a few minutes onto the bedclothes that were still strewn across the rug, putting her hands on her belly. She almost drummed a tune on her flat stomach as she spoke to herself.

"What makes sense? The bedroom cupboards are all empty. You wouldn't put something as fragile as a photo album in the kitchen or any of the bathrooms. The main dining room and living room cupboards are empty. And I nearly broke my back trying to scramble up into the attic space."

Matteo couldn't help himself. He started to laugh. Maybe it was being overtired. Maybe it was just frustration that he couldn't get away from the one place he didn't want to be. Or maybe it was the sight of Phoebe's legs hanging from the attic and doing her best impression of a spider trying to cling to any surface.

She opened her eyes and stared up at him. "Matteo Bianchi, are you laughing at me?"

Before he had a chance to answer she sat bolt upright

again and smacked her hand off her forehead. "Oh, my goodness. We're idiots. Complete idiots."

Matteo shook his head. "What? What is it?"

Phoebe spread her arms wide. "What was the one place you know your family didn't have any immediate plans for?"

Matteo shook his head again. He was still tired. He'd been tempted to lie down on one of the beds that Phoebe had already dressed upstairs, regardless of whether it would ruin the look of the room or not.

Phoebe jumped up. Literally, jumped up onto her feet, a wide smile across her face. "We're dummies," she declared before spinning around. "Here, Matteo. *Here.* The library. The place that was going to remain undisturbed. The place that children probably wouldn't play, and the renovations wouldn't touch." She ran over and flicked the main light switch, flooding the room with light.

It was like being hit by a thunderbolt. Of course. *Of course.*

Phoebe had already made her way over to the shelves. She wagged her finger at him. "It's time for us to stop sniggering like naughty school kids at the ancient sex manuals and look for the real prize. A red album. It has to be here."

Phoebe climbed up the shaky rolling steps and started to look at the top shelves. She pointed downwards. "Let's be methodical about this. You look at the shelves underneath me."

Matteo nodded. His eyes swept along the shelves. A lot of the books were far too thick to be a photo album. Most of them were the wrong color. He pulled out a few, checking they really were books, then pushing them back onto the shelves.

"Right," came Phoebe's authoritative voice from above him. "Push me along a bit."

He looked up and pulled a face at her.

"What? There's no point in me climbing up and down, when you can just push me along."

"I think you're enjoying this a little too much."

She shrugged and gave him a little smile. "Maybe. But push me along anyhow."

The ladder squeaked and shook as he wheeled her along. "Don't get used to this," he murmured.

She laughed above him and his stomach gave a little flip. The horrible dread and associations he'd always had about this place didn't seem quite so bad when Phoebe was around. Five minutes later—after she'd got used to ordering him around—Phoebe let out a squeal.

"I think I've got it!"

Matteo jumped back, stopping at the bottom of the steps. Phoebe spun around above him, clutching a red album in one hand. Excitement seemed to bubble from her. He lifted his arms up toward her. It just seemed so natural. So easy. And Phoebe didn't hesitate—she let him lift her down the steps.

The album was in her hands. It looked old. She flicked open the front page then stopped and stared at him. "Oh, I'm sorry. Do you want to do this yourself?"

He hesitated. Part of him absolutely did.

But part of him absolutely didn't.

All of a sudden the lights in the library seemed too bright.

"Give me a second." He walked over and flipped them off. Somehow it seemed safer to be in the flickering firelight. "Let's sit down," he said.

Phoebe nodded and walked back over, sitting down in front of the fireplace with the album on her lap. She

waited until he joined her, then opened the first page
again.

There was no photo. Instead his parents' names were
written in calligraphy.

*15th June 1980*
*Roberto Matteo Bianchi and Lucianna Maria Aquino*

His mouth suddenly felt dry and he was conscious
of Phoebe's eyes on him. He couldn't remember ever
looking at his parents' wedding album before. He was
sure he'd seen one wedding picture. His father had kept
one in a frame, hidden away in his study for years. But
the rest? Matteo had never seen them.

He flicked over the next page and caught his breath.
His mother. So young. She was twenty-two when she
got married. She was sitting in her wedding dress in
front of her dressing table looking suitably nervous for
a young bride.

Her dress was an Italian lace overlay over a white
bodice. It was simple. Round necked and short sleeved.
It cinched in at the waist, with the skirt flaring out.
Her dark brown curls cascaded over one shoulder and
clutched in her hand a bunch of white lilies surrounded
by baby's breath. His mother had always loved those.
They'd decorated the house frequently.

Phoebe touched the plastic covering the photo. "Her
dress is beautiful," she murmured. Matteo licked his
lips. He'd always known that Brianna was the spitting
image of their mother, but never had it been so apparent.
They could almost be the same person. That thought
was enough to send a cold chill down his spine.

Phoebe flicked the page. The wedding album was
filled with all the usual pictures. Matteo's mother with

her own father, looking suitably proud. A gaggle of bridesmaids, all dressed in wide pale pink dresses. A whole host of relatives that even Matteo wasn't entirely sure of.

But then Phoebe flicked the page again and there was his father. His eyes full of joy and life. It was like a fist closing around Matteo's heart.

It wasn't that his father had spent the rest of his life miserable. There had been the odd glimmer of spark and happiness. But the truth was, those moments had been few and far between. After the death of his mother, his father had focused all his energy and attention on business. He'd been ruthless. Sometimes heartless about the decisions he'd made.

He'd never been a bad father. He'd never ignored his children. He'd just been a little...vacant.

Seeing this picture of him so full of life and joy almost wrenched the heart from Matteo's chest. Phoebe was oblivious. She had a dreamy smile on her face as she flicked the pages. The next showed his mother and father clasping hands at the altar and exchanging vows. The love and devotion was painted on their faces for all the world to see.

Phoebe let out a little wistful sigh. "How gorgeous," she whispered.

The twisting sensation in his chest stopped. He looked at the picture again with new eyes. It *was* gorgeous. It was a moment in time—a moment to remember. He lifted his fingers to the page. "I think I'd quite like to copy that photograph," he said, his voice heavy with emotion.

"You've lost them both now, haven't you?"

The emotions were bubbling up inside him. He'd been feeling anger—despair. Everything about this place overwhelmed him with sadness. But just that single comment. And just the chance to sit down and look through these photos was helping him to take stock.

His parents on their wedding day. So much happiness. So much hope. They'd lived a good life together. His father's business had flourished. His mother had always been adventurous. She'd relished the move to the United States. She'd loved New York and been happy to plan to bring her children up here.

She'd been happy. She'd adored her husband, and looked forward to a lifetime together. Matteo's stomach gave a little twist. But fate and misfortune had cut that short. He lowered his head. If he'd raised the alarm... if he'd realized she wasn't sleeping...

Phoebe turned toward him, her rose scent drifting up around him. Her face was only inches away from his. Their bodies were so close. His arm was resting on the floor, but placed between her arm and her body. Just by looking at the album they'd practically found themselves intertwined. Was this fate? Or was this fortune?

It was almost as if all his instincts about Phoebe fell into place at once. She lifted her head, her nose brushing against his chin, and reached up and touched his cheek.

It was the smallest of movements, with a whole lot of heart.

"I think it would be beautiful as a black and white canvas," she whispered. "Something to look at, and remember." She paused for a second then added, "We all should remember the things that are precious to us."

He looked up and met her gaze. In the flickering firelight it was possible he'd never seen a woman look quite so beautiful. Phoebe might be dressed in the most casual of clothes, her hair might show remnants of dust, but her light brown skin glowed, and her dark eyes pulled him in.

There was something there. Something he'd never experienced before. A connection. A feeling. A sincerity.

The timing might be wrong. The circumstances might be less than ideal. But he couldn't help his instincts. As the world burst into life outside and fireworks filled the air to celebrate the New Year, Matteo bent his head and met her soft lips.

There was no shock. No disdain. Phoebe's lips were as sweet and inviting as he could have hoped for. The kiss was gentle—sweet. She returned it, her lips parting ever so slightly, encouraging him.

His hand reached up and tangled in her curls, pulling her head closer to his. She let out a little sigh and it was almost his undoing. It would be so easy to continue. So easy to let this progress. They were already on the floor. The bedclothes were scattered around them. He could just pull her on top of him, or slip his hand under the pink top. He could see her gentle curves, and the temptation to touch them was overwhelming.

But, for the first time in his life, Matteo didn't let his natural instincts set the pace. Instead, he swallowed, and reluctantly let his lips part from hers. He could still taste her, and he'd never felt so hungry for more. Every part of his body urged him to continue.

But he took a deep breath and rested his forehead against hers, his hand still tangled in her hair. Phoebe's breathing was labored and heavy, just like his. But she didn't push for anything else. She seemed happy to take a moment too. Her chest was rising and falling in his eye line as they stayed for a few minutes with their heads together.

Everything felt too new. Too raw. Did he even know what he was doing here?

"Happy New Year," he said softly. "At least I'm guessing that's why we can still hear fireworks."

"There are fireworks outside? I thought they were inside." Her sparkling dark eyes met his gaze and she smiled. "Wow," she said huskily.

He let out a laugh. "Wow," he repeated.

Her hand was hesitant, reaching up, then stopping, then reaching up again. She finally rested it against his chest, the fingertips pausing on one of the buttons of his shirt.

His mind was willing her to unfasten it. But she just let it sit there. The warmth of her fingertips permeating through his designer shirt. He could sense she wanted to say something, and it made him want to stumble and fill the silence.

For the first time in his life, Matteo Bianchi was out of his depth. It was a completely alien feeling for him. In matters of the opposite sex he was always in charge, always the one to initiate things, or, more likely, finish them. He'd never been unsure of himself, never uncomfortable.

But from the minute he'd met this woman with a warm smile and thoughtful heart, he just hadn't known how to deal with her. She had a way of looking at him as he answered a question that let him know his blasé, offhand remarks didn't wash with her. She didn't push. She didn't need to. He was quite sure that, if she wanted to, Phoebe Gates would take no prisoners. But the overwhelming aura from Phoebe was one of warmth, of kindness and sincerity. And it was making his heart beat quicker every minute.

She pulled back and blew out a long breath, watching him with her steady eyes. She glanced down at her watch. "Yup—two minutes past. I guess we missed the big countdown."

It would be so easy. So easy to make a mistake here. So easy to do everything wrong, just because it might feel a little right. "I don't think we did," he said softly.

For a few seconds they just sat and breathed. Her fingers intertwined with his. His sallow skin with her light coffee skin. They seemed to match perfectly.

"Give me a minute," he said as he jumped to his feet. She looked a little surprised but didn't speak. There was almost a roaring in his ears as he raced first up the stairs to grab some pillows and another set of blankets, then he grabbed his car keys to head out to the car.

He shook his head as he glanced at the icy driveway, taking careful steps to find what he was looking for from the glove box of the car. A few minutes later he was back in the library.

Phoebe looked a little self-conscious now, tugging at her sleeves and biting her bottom lip. Her eyes widened at the pillows. But Matteo knew exactly what he was doing. He kept things easy. He kept things relaxed as he threw the pillows on the floor. "It's late. I figured we're both tired by now. Here, I thought the cushions might be a little uncomfortable. You're right, the rest of the house is just too cold. So, we'll camp down here tonight and sort things out tomorrow. I even have a surprise." He couldn't help but smile as a frown creased Phoebe's brow.

"What surprise?"

He pulled the candy bars from behind his back and tossed them toward her. "Don't let it be said that I don't have any vices. I keep a secret stash in my glove box. Don't you remember as a child all the best movies had kids having midnight feasts? Think of this as our own version."

The tension in Phoebe's shoulders dissipated a little. She stared at the four candy bars scattered on the bed-clothes in front of her and looked up and gave him a little smile. "Do I get first pick?"

"Always," he said as he plumped down beside her. "I'm a gentleman, didn't you know that?"

There was a pause. A second where their gazes meshed. An understanding. There was no pressure here. There were no uncomfortable thoughts. He wasn't going to pursue something. He had too much respect for her for that.

He wanted things to be on her terms. Strictly speaking, Phoebe was an employee. It didn't matter if it was only for a few weeks.

Then, there was the fact they were currently stranded here. Above all he wanted Phoebe to feel safe around him. He might hate the fact he was going to have to spend the night in this house—but Phoebe being here made everything a whole lot easier.

The truth was, he probably wouldn't have found the album without her. And if she hadn't been here he would certainly have made the foolhardy decision to try and travel back on the icy roads rather than stay here alone.

That simple statement seemed to have done the trick. Phoebe grabbed one of the pillows and put it next to her. It seemed that bunking down in front of the fire wasn't so scary after all. She gave a slow nod and held her hand over one bar, then another. "Decisions, deci-sions," she teased. "I'd hate to make the wrong choice."

"I'm not sure you ever make the wrong choice." The words were out before he had time to think about them. "Look what you've done with the house so far," he added quickly. Trying to keep things simple.

Phoebe's eyebrows were raised, but she lowered them again and closed her hand over the chocolate and caramel bar.

"Thank goodness," he sighed as he whipped the raspberry and dark chocolate from under her nose.

Phoebe held up her bar. "If only we had coffee to go with these."

He held up his hands. "I'm good, but I'm not that good."

Phoebe took a bite of her chocolate bar, then settled her blankets out. She gave him a cute smile. "Who says you're good?"

# CHAPTER FIVE

SHE FELT FUGGY. Was that even a real word?

"Ms. Gates? Ms. Gates, are you here?"

Her mouth was dry and uncomfortable and her back ached. But something was warm. Something felt cozy. It was a sensation she hadn't felt in a long time.

That ease of someone close behind, their body next to hers, a relaxed arm resting over her stomach, and warm breath near her neck.

"Ms. Gates, are you here?" There was a creak. A noise.

Phoebe sat bolt upright. Oh, no. Oh...what?

The joiner was standing at the door of the library. "Oops, excuse me. I saw your car outside and just thought I'd check you were safe." His eyes fixed behind her, his cheeks flamed and he shook his head and backed out the door. "Sorry."

"No, Al." Phoebe jumped to her feet and ran to the door. "I'm sorry. We got stranded here last night with the roads. I couldn't get the car to move." She frowned. "Wait a minute. How did you get here? How did you get in?"

Al shrugged. "The gritters have been out since three a.m. Most of the roads are passable now. The caretaker met me outside. Turned out he'd some rock salt and put it on the driveway this morning." Al glanced at his watch. "I take it the others will be here any minute."

"They will?" Phoebe turned on her heel and dashed back into the library. Matteo was already on his feet, tugging at his completely wrinkled shirt and trousers. Thank goodness they were both fully dressed.

Her mind did a bit of a backspin. Things could have totally gone in another direction last night. Part of her was glad it hadn't, and part of her was secretly disappointed. How would she have felt this morning if things had progressed?

She'd kissed him. She'd kissed Matteo Bianchi. *Her boss.*

And he'd kissed her back.

It was the first time she'd kissed someone since Jason had died. And the wash of guilt was overwhelming.

What was worse—she hadn't felt it last night. It hadn't even crossed her mind last night. What kind of person did that make her? To forget her dead fiancé after three years at the glint of an Italian man's eyes? Her body started to tremble.

She'd never felt ready. Never felt ready to move on. To take the first step. Her few dates had been disasters. But this had been unexpected—unplanned. What was she thinking?

Matteo looked confused as she walked back in. "You have people working on New Year's Day?"

She tried to gather her thoughts. Matteo seemed a bit uncomfortable. Maybe he was having regrets too. But this was business. This was work. She replied quickly. "Actually, *you* do. And you're paying them a big bonus for doing it. This is a rush job—remember?"

He didn't look particularly happy. He tied his shoes and stared disdainfully at the crumpled bedclothes on the floor. Phoebe winced. Yesterday, they had been smooth and pristine on the beds upstairs. In the cold light of day, it looked as if the adults in the room had been romping all night.

She bent down and scooped them up into her arms. Last thing she wanted was the rest of the people working in the house to see this. It made her feel like some kind of naughty school kid—even though nothing had really happened.

"Let me take care of these," she said quickly to Matteo as she disappeared back out of the door.

It only took a second to realize her mistake. A waft of his aftershave floated up from the blankets and her footsteps faltered. That kiss. How could she forget that kiss? The one that made her float toward the ceiling and never come back down. Just that memory made her heart rate quicken all over again. She kept walking to the kitchen, trying not to rethink things, ignoring the way that all the little hairs on her arms had just stood on end.

Jason. She should be thinking about Jason. Her breathing stuttered along with her footsteps. For the last year, the memories that used to be so vivid had started to fade a little. But right now, that just made her feel a million times worse. Was she going to forget about him completely? Her brain was so muddled. First her mother being sick and needing treatment, then the hospital bills, followed by the dream job, and the mysterious Italian. It was no wonder she couldn't think straight.

By the time she reached the kitchen she realized she was crazy. The washer wasn't plumbed in yet. She couldn't do the laundry and wash his smell out the bed-clothes. She sighed. She didn't want to leave them in the kitchen where they could get even dirtier as the kitchen refit continued, so she turned back to head to the stairs.

Matteo was striding toward her, the album under his arm. He almost tripped when he saw her—it was clear he'd been planning on heading straight out of the door.

She swallowed again and felt a little surge of anger. The rattling kind that meant she really needed her morning dose of caffeine. That was it. The first thing she was doing today was going out to buy a coffeepot somewhere. He opened his mouth to speak, but nothing came out.

She gave him her best smile. "Let me know if there's anything specific you want me to do in the house."

Bland. Idiotic. It was the best she could do. She felt like the high school girl who the Prom King had kissed by mistake. Not exactly the best feeling in the world.

He licked his lips as that floppy brown hair of his fell over his eyes. If she had a razor right now, she would shave it clean off.

He glanced around. What was he looking at? He was surrounded by cream-colored walls. "You seem to have everything under control here. Maybe next week we should talk about plans for Rome?"

Her tongue glued itself to the top of her mouth. Rome. No. No. No.

That was a plane ride away. Probably more than one.

It was clear that he took her silence as agreement. He walked past. "Drop me an email when the house is ready and I'll contact the realtor."

She pressed her lips together as the surge of anger flooded her veins. Would it be wrong to push her employer straight out of the front door? She let her feet stay rooted to the spot, with her arms tightly clutching the bedclothes until she heard the door close behind him.

Nothing. No, *Thanks for last night*. No, *That was nice*. No, *Will I call you?* And definitely no, *I'm sorry*.

It was like being dismissed. Being ignored.

She stamped up the curving stairs, every step a little more forceful. Was this what Matteo did with women? Kiss them mercilessly, then just walk away?

Tears burned in her eyes. She was overreacting. She knew she was. But she couldn't fight the wave of hurt that burned through her.

He wasn't to know that it was her first kiss since her fiancé had died. He wasn't to know that even though she'd tried to get back out in the dating game, her heart just hadn't been in it.

He wasn't to know that last night, for the first time in three years, she'd actually *felt* something again. A spark. A glimmer of hope.

It was as if the cloud that had settled on her shoulders had finally started to lift. It was as if a stream of sunlight was starting to poke through.

Before, she'd always felt guilty. Guilty she was on a date. Guilty she was out again. It had never felt quite right. She had never felt quite ready.

So why did now have to be the time for her to feel ready? Why did the first guy who sent tingles down her spine and kissed her as she'd never been kissed before have to be her boss?

Matteo had lit a flame that had been tempered for so long.

Last night had felt so right. Why was he acting as if it were so wrong?

Maybe she was crazy—a whole world of crazy. How could she possibly even consider putting her heart out there again? It had been broken in the worst kind of way.

There was no way she could consider letting herself be hurt like that again.

She dumped the bedclothes in the corner of one of the rooms. She didn't care how messy they were. They could stay like that until the washer was finally plumbed in.

She pressed her lips together and put her hands on her hips. Right now she was so mad it was easy to push the other stuff out of her head. The Rome stuff. She would find an excuse. A reason not to be able to go.

He would still pay her for her work here. That would surely be enough to put a dent in the bill for her mother's medical care. The very last thing she wanted to do was spend any more time in an enclosed space with Matteo Bianchi—the guy who could kiss her, then treat her as if she'd never existed.

She looked around and lifted her chin. He wanted this house dressed?

Then, boy, he could have it.

"Mr. Bianchi?" Constance, his new, efficient, but very nervous PA was hovering by the door. She had a habit of shifting from foot to foot. At first he'd thought the stilettos that she favored were either too high, or too uncomfortable. But he'd quickly realized it was just a nervous habit.

He barely looked up. "Yes?"

There was silence. So he did look up—just in time to see her bite her bottom lip.

"What is it?"

She took a few tentative steps into the room, a piece of paper in her hand. She held it out rather shakily. "I just thought you should know that, in the last few days, there's been…extensive billing to the business account."

He frowned, not quite sure what she meant. "What?" He took the piece of paper and studied it.

His eyes just about popped out of their sockets as he stood up so quickly his chair fell to the floor behind him with a crash. Constance was out the room in a flash; apparently she could move quicker than a speeding bullet—even in stilettos.

Matteo started walking toward the door but was blocked by a figure in the doorway. Brianna's eyebrows were raised and her arms folded across her chest. It seemed as if her belly got bigger every single day. "Well, somebody's in a good mood."

"Leave it, Brianna. I have to go." He sighed, as he had to stop walking. "Any chance of letting me past?"

Brianna shook her head. She was dressed more casually than normal, her dark hair tied up in a ponytail. "Not until I know what's going on."

He held up the printout for her to see. "What's going on is that my interior designer has just gone stir crazy!"

Brianna screwed up her eyes and looked at the figure at the bottom of the page. "Wow," she said as a smile spread from ear to ear.

"That's all you can say—wow?"

She shook her head. "Actually, I can say a whole lot more." She gave Matteo her special gaze. The one that clearly meant he was in trouble. "I don't care what she spends. We've agreed we want to sell the house—and the house is decades out of date. As far as I'm concerned, as long as it sells, the interior design bill doesn't matter." She shook her head and stepped closer to her brother. "Oh, no. What I'm interested in, is what *you've* done."

"What's that supposed to mean?"

Brianna tapped him on the chest. "You think I'm stupid? First week you went shopping with her at the warehouse. She bought a whole host of things—but nothing outrageous." Brianna scanned the piece of paper again. "But this list? *These* purchases?" She started to laugh. "This is the sign of a woman scorned." She shook her head again. "I so want to meet this woman. Look how wound up you are—I haven't seen you like this in…" She frowned and met his gaze. "In forever."

Her voice softened. "What happened, Matteo?"

Matteo paused. He'd spent the last four days cringing inside and out. He'd handled things badly. He'd actually spent a beautiful night with a gorgeous, sensitive woman, then acted like the town fool the next morning. Matteo had never been the tongue-tied adolescent before, so finding himself turned into one that morning had been a completely alien experience.

It was obvious he'd hurt her feelings—even though that had never been his intention. And it was clear that now she was just letting him know.

He stepped backwards. Every day Brianna looked more like their mother. And every day it reminded him of exactly what had happened. It seemed as if his stomach had been in a permanent knot since Brianna had announced her pregnancy. He couldn't tell her just how worried he was. She'd already had a few little hiccups. Borderline blood pressure and a little bleeding in the early stages. For a single man, he'd quickly learned more about pregnancy than he'd ever wanted to.

Her gaze narrowed. It was almost as if she could partly read his mind. "Matteo, did you find it—did you find the album?"

He gave a nod and walked back to the desk, sliding open one of the drawers and pulling out the red album. He hesitated. "Phoebe helped me find it."

Brianna walked swiftly around the desk, righting Matteo's chair and sitting down with the album in front of her. She rested her hands on the album tentatively. "Have you looked at this?"

He pressed his lips together, then walked back to the door, picking up something behind it. It was a canvas. He'd listened to Phoebe. He spun it around and Brianna let out a little whimper. She was on her feet instantly. "Oh, my goodness." She reached her hands out to gently touch the canvas. "This is beautiful. They look so happy. It's just so, so..." Tears brimmed in her eyes. "How on earth?" Her voice tailed off.

Matteo's heart was heavy in his chest. "It's one of the photos in the album. Phoebe suggested getting it made into a black and white canvas." He gave a nod of acknowledgement. "She has a good eye."

Tears started to flow down Brianna's cheeks. "Oh, she *so* does." She looked over her shoulder. "It's one from the album?"

He nodded and she walked back over and sat down, spending the next five minutes flicking slowly through the pictures. He couldn't speak—only watch as his sister went through the same experience that he had. When she reached the last page she closed the album and held it close to her chest. She stayed that way for a few seconds then stood up and walked over, wrapping her arms around his neck.

"Thank you," she whispered. "Thank you for going back to the house and finding this for me."

Her swollen stomach was pressed against him and her baby decided to give a little kick. He jumped back in surprise as Brianna smiled and put her hand on her stomach.

"My little one is grateful too. Now, he or she gets

to see pictures of their past. Pictures of the people we love."

Matteo gave a slow nod. He knew she was right. But everything just seemed so raw right now. Brianna stepped forward again. "Are you going to tell me what happened?"

He felt a chill all over his body. Of course Brianna wasn't talking about their mother. She couldn't possibly know. His brain tried to rationalize. "About the album?"

She reached down and picked up the piece of paper. "About this? What did you do to her, Matteo? What did you do to upset the girl who has finally put a little sparkle in your eyes?"

He blinked. "What?"

"You heard me. You like her. I know you do. You've been different these past few weeks."

He threw up his hands in frustration. "I'm different because I have things to deal with. We have two houses to sell."

Brianna gave a nod of acknowledgement. "We have. And I thought you might find this stressful. You were the oldest. You saw much more than Vittore or I did. But..." she looked up at him "...you've been better than I thought." She took the crumpled paper from his hand. "And I think it's because of this. I think it's because of her." She glanced at the figure at the bottom again and smiled and shook her head. "And it looks like you better start apologizing soon. Otherwise it will be a *very* long flight to Rome."

Phoebe looked around. She'd thrown herself into finishing this place, bringing down some clothes from her apartment and even spending the last few nights here.

She'd hired extra staff and yet another cleaning crew to achieve everything she wanted.

The last person had left half an hour ago. So, she'd taken some time to shower and change out of her grubby clothes into something bright, something fresh, and probably far too cold for a winter's day. But Phoebe didn't care. There was a paycheck on the horizon. Her bright yellow dress was a signal of triumph.

The drapes were hung, the light fittings all changed, the beds remade. The recovered chairs and sofas were exquisite. The leather was soft and tactile, the muted shades suited the rooms perfectly. All the finishing touches were in place. The lamps, the vases, cushions and throws. New prints and mirrors hung on freshly painted walls and light streamed in every window.

She walked from room to room, lighting candles along the way. Orange and lemon in the main rooms, clean linen candles in the bedrooms, and lavender and rose in the newly finished kitchen. She wiped a cloth across the deep white Belfast sinks. They were gorgeous. Just perfect in the old-style kitchen.

There was an aura about this place. Something special. She'd felt it the moment she'd arrived. And now, finally, she was finished.

She pulled her phone from her pocket and stared at it a few seconds. The realtor had already visited this morning, measuring rooms and taking hundreds of photos. Her over-eagerness at the possibility of a sale was palpable. Phoebe looked around. How much would a place like this be worth? It had to be over fifty million dollars. It *had* to be.

Everyone had left now. She was entirely alone. The scented candles started to gently fill the air around her.

She drifted back down the corridor to the main entrance and that gorgeous atrium and curved staircase.

Images floated into her mind of her favorite childhood cartoon movie. She started to hum one of the tunes and dance a little around the bottom of the stairs. All she needed was a yellow ball gown. Her yellow dress only reached her knees, but it was floaty enough. She lifted her hands as if she had a magical partner and started to waltz around as the humming changed to singing. Phoebe had never really been a singer, but who could hear? Right now, this was her palace. In here, her mother had never been sick. There were no bills. Jason had never died.

She started to dance up the stairs. That was the favorite part of the movie for her. She didn't need a partner. It was much easier if it was all just in her head. She'd probably never get the chance to do something like this again. She was going to just enjoy every minute.

She couldn't help but smile. Hopefully whoever bought his place would appreciate it as much as she did.

"Is this what you always do when left alone?"

The voice cut through her thoughts and made her stumble. Her foot slid on the stairs and she fell—straight into a strong pair of arms.

Instantly, she was defensive. His skin was next to hers. The smell of his aftershave enveloped her. She pushed back. Heat rushing to her face. She'd been dancing around like a five-year-old. *Singing.* And he'd seen her. He'd caught her in the act.

There was a glimmer of a smile on his face. But she couldn't return it. She was still angry at the way he'd treated her so indifferently.

She'd played on those few seconds over and over. What she *should* have said. What she *should* have done.

So many different scenarios that all added up to the same thing.

She needed to get away from Matteo Bianchi as soon as possible.

Matteo must have noticed her expression because he didn't even wait for a response to his previous question. "We need to talk."

There was something in his tone. Something that sent a little shiver down her spine.

She tilted her chin up toward him and held out her hands. "What about? Haven't you seen—I'm done here. The house is finished. The realtor's been. All that happens now is that you pay me."

She was being bold. She'd never been so forward with a client before. But then again, a client had never kissed her before. Or was it she that had kissed him?

Her insides turned over. *Who had kissed who?*

Something flickered in his eyes. Almost as if he were assessing the situation. Or assessing *her.* Something was off. Almost as if…was it hurt? A wave of pain? Why on earth would Matteo feel like that? What was it with this guy? Trying to figure him out was driving her crazy.

Matteo looked around. "Let's take a walk through. Show me what you've done." There was a waver in his voice.

She blinked. He hadn't even reacted to her almost cheeky remarks. She spun around. "Absolutely, let's start in the kitchen."

It didn't matter that her blood was currently racing through her veins. It didn't matter that she really wanted to limp on the stumbled ankle. She was proud of her work. She'd done a good job—she knew she had.

She could do a walk-through. Then she could see about getting paid.

\* \* \*

Matteo's heart was somewhere between his mouth and the pit of his stomach. She couldn't know. She just couldn't.

But when he'd seen Phoebe twirling on the stairs he'd had a complete flashback to his mother. It didn't matter that they looked entirely different. Matteo's mother's long dark hair and sallow skin was entirely different from Phoebe's springy curls and pale coffee complexion. But it was the essence of them that seemed the same, that sent that surge of familiar emotions sweeping through his body. The life that was in them. Or used to be.

Phoebe's bright yellow dress was beautiful. A little unusual for this time of year. Maybe she had plans? Maybe she had somewhere else to go today? His stomach gave another flip as he followed her into the kitchen. Could she have a date?

Why was the coffee he'd drunk an hour ago suddenly gurgling around inside him?

It was amazing how a few subtle changes could transform a place. The large Belfast sinks were definitely the focal point. Phoebe gave him a minute to look around. "You'll see the sinks are now finished, the cream kitchen units have been revamped, some have been moved around. The walls are now a pale yellow to add a hint of color." She ran her hand along the new countertop. "And the dark wooden countertop is just the perfect finish, don't you agree?"

The way she phrased her words was almost as if she was challenging him to disagree. But he couldn't. The kitchen looked impressive. As did the laundry room, and the storage room.

Phoebe led him through to the main room. "You

can see how the color palette worked out," she said. The drapes at the window were striped, the sofas and chairs covered in soft gray leather, with a large gray and yellow rug dressing the light oak floor. Most other houses he'd visited over the years were almost bland. Everything either white or cream.

But Phoebe had a good understanding of color. The room was light enough to still enhance its size, but the color added something else—a sense of life. A sense of harmony. With a citrus scent in the air.

He pressed his lips together as she led him through to the sitting room at the back of the house. This room had glass doors that opened out to Mecox Bay. Here, the drapes were minimal, tied back to let the choppy waters of the bay be the focal point. The colors in here were slightly different. More pale blue than gray. It was almost as if, instead of dressing the house, Phoebe had been dressing the bay. She understood even more than he'd given her credit for.

She flicked on a small lamp in the corner. He sucked in a breath. "Is that a Tiffany?"

She laughed. "Of course not. I didn't spend *that* much money. It's a reproduction. But I thought it helped. There's very little color in this room, just cream and pale blue. Can you imagine, at night, sitting here, staring out over the dark bay, and flicking on this lamp, having the reflections of the blue, yellow and red glass across the walls? It would be almost magical."

For a few seconds, Matteo held his breath. He could almost picture it in his head. The trouble was that picture seemed homely. Warm. Inviting. Things he just couldn't associate with this house anymore.

He kept his voice steady. "Interesting. I think you've done a good job in the house, so far."

Phoebe made the tiniest movement. Did she flinch? Her face appeared a bit pinched. He'd thought he'd just complimented her work, but maybe not.

She swept past him and kept going. "Let's move up to the second floor."

They moved back out to the staircase, and Phoebe practically ran up it—obviously trying to shake the memories of being caught dancing on it earlier.

The bedrooms were all finished to a high standard, each with a few unique or quirky items just to personalize the rooms. The bathrooms were similar. Sparkling white, with some yellow or pale blue accessories.

Phoebe walked at speed, moving from room to room and talking constantly. Her work was impeccable. He'd already had a call from the realtor, who had gushed and complimented him so much he'd actually wondered at one stage if she was going to offer to have his baby. The realtor loved the house and had hinted that she predicted a sale would be quick.

"This is obviously the master bedroom so it's been dressed a little more demurely than the others. Again, since the view is a pivotal part of this room I've kept the color palette sedated."

She was tugging at a little bit of hair at the nape of her neck. *She's nervous.* Of course she was. The last time he'd seen her they'd been kissing.

His fingers crackled the paper in his pocket. He'd come here to question her about the expenses. But, as he walked from room to room, he could see exactly where every single cent had been spent. The house wasn't completely transformed. But it *was* different.

It felt different. Even to him. There was no question he was still haunted by the memories of his mother. But at least now he could start to dissociate himself from this place. Phoebe had made everything look new. It even smelled different.

Phoebe was still talking. Still tugging at her hair. "So, there's only a few other rooms. But I don't think you need to see them." She turned to face him.

"As you can see, my job here is complete." She gave him a bright smile that seemed forced. "Maybe we should talk about my payment?"

He raised his eyebrows. "Maybe we should talk about Rome? That is our agreement. Complete both houses, not just one. I can arrange plane tickets for tomorrow. Once I've shown you the house, and introduced you to the staff, I can leave."

Phoebe visibly blanched but Matteo continued, his hands in his pockets as he walked around the room. "You've done an excellent job. The look of the house is much improved." He gave a little smile. "Even though you might have broke the bank this last week." He moved over to the window and stared out at the bay. Even in the middle of winter, the choppy sea was a mixture of blues and grays. There were a few boats out on the bay. The view was entirely spectacular and would probably be the selling point of this house. "I think it's time to move forward."

He turned back around to face Phoebe. She was staring at the floor, fumbling with her hands. "I think that Rome might not work. It would make more sense for you to deal with an Italian interior designer who has a good idea of the best selling points for the Italian market. And the best tradesmen to work with. I have absolutely no grasp of the Italian language. I think I'd be far more of a hindrance than a help."

Matteo frowned and stepped forward. "But we had an agreement. I asked you to do both houses for me."

He dug his hands a little deeper in his pockets. "And wouldn't a house in Rome be good for your CV? As well as the house in the Hamptons?" Matteo wasn't stupid. He knew exactly how much kudos doing this house would give her. He couldn't understand why she wouldn't want to also have an international mansion on her portfolio.

Phoebe still refused to meet his gaze. She was shaking her head the whole time. Did she even realize she was doing it?

He pulled his phone from his jacket pocket. "Let me book the flights. When you see the house, you'll love it." He started flicking through the contacts in his phone.

"No." The word was almost a whisper.

His head jerked back up. "What?"

"No." The word was now a little less shaky. She lifted her head and finally met his gaze again. It was almost as if she were struggling to get her breath.

"What are you talking about?" He moved even closer. He was starting to get annoyed. "I employed you to dress both houses, the one here and the one in Rome."

"I know that…" she started, "but…"

"But what?" He threw up his hands. "Why on earth are you stalling? We had an agreement."

"I… I… I…"

There was something about the way she was stuck for words. That didn't seem normal for Phoebe. Her eyes filled with tears as he watched her.

He stepped over and touched her bare arm. "What on earth is wrong?"

She glanced down at his hand on her arm and he frowned. Something shot through his head and he was flooded with panic. "Is this about us? Is this about this kiss?"

Darn it. He knew he'd handled things badly—probably closest to a hormonal teenager. It was ridiculous. He was a grown man with a world of experience in kissing women.

But he'd never kissed a girl like Phoebe. He'd never kissed a girl who'd made him feel as if the fireworks going off outside were actually part of him. He'd never wanted to continue a kiss more than he'd wanted to that night. But it had been an impulsive thing. A lapse of judgement.

So why couldn't he get it out of his head?

Phoebe met his gaze again. "It's nothing to do with the kiss." She sounded exasperated, and a little bit sad. "It's just a whole other part of my life that I'm just not ready to deal with."

Matteo pulled back a little. "Phoebe, what is going on? Is something wrong?" The mark on her face the other day? Was this something to do with that? It was amazing how instantly protective he still felt about her.

She took a deep breath and he let his hand fall from her arm. Physical contact between them wasn't a good idea. "No, it's nothing like that."

He was getting impatient. "Then I'll see you at JFK airport tomorrow. The flight takes around eight and a half hours and it's a red eye. Dress comfortably."

"It's just…"

"Phoebe, I don't have time for this." He couldn't hide his frustration. Timing was everything. February was a crucial time for his business. He couldn't be distracted. He needed to deal with the house in Rome now. "I was clear. I offered you a quarter of a million dollars to dress two houses for me. One in the Hamptons. One in Rome. You agreed." He shrugged. "I don't take kindly to people who renege on business agreements. There are…consequences."

She blinked and he could see her brain trying to interpret those words. "You mean if I don't come to Rome, you won't pay me?" The shock on her face was clear.

"We had a deal, Phoebe. You keep your end of the bargain. I keep mine. I like to deal with professionals. I thought that's what you were." His eyes swept up and down her. Taking in the yellow dress and nude heels. "Maybe I was wrong."

Her words were strained. Her jaw clenched. "I am a professional. My job here proves it. This house will sell easily."

He walked straight over to her. Closer than he intended. He could see every inch of her smooth clear skin. The mascara outlining her long dark lashes. The hint of red on her lips. Her very kissable lips. "Your professionalism is proved once you complete the job."

He met her dark gaze. He couldn't read what was going on in those strong brown eyes. Phoebe's eyes had always flashed a multitude of emotions. Today? It was almost as if a set of shutters had closed across them. They were angry. Detached.

She tilted her chin up toward him. He could see the tiny pulse at the base of her throat. "What time do you need me?"

"I'll have a car pick you up at six p.m."

"Fine." She turned on her heel, her yellow dress swirling around her knees, as she walked out of the room.

# CHAPTER SIX

SHE HADN'T EVEN met his gaze since she'd climbed in the car.

Pride and terror wouldn't let her. But as the car had got closer and closer to the airport she could almost hear the tattoo of her heartbeat against her chest.

The worst thing had been her mother. When she'd told her she was going to Rome to do a job, her mother's eyes had filled with tears and she'd cupped Phoebe's face and told her how proud she was of her. And how it was time.

All the words of fear and anxiety that had been ready to spill out of her mouth had halted instantly. Her mother was feeling well. Her treatments were finished and she was under instruction to rest for the next month. Phoebe couldn't use her mother's illness as an excuse not to go. Her mother would never forgive her.

Matteo's secretary had contacted Phoebe for her passport number and checked them both in online. As soon as they'd stepped out of the car the noise of the airport had overwhelmed her. The constant whoosh of planes taking off and landing. The chatter of people arriving or leaving. The thumping of cases. The toot of taxis.

It was like a roaring in her ears.

Matteo, of course, seemed oblivious. He steered her

to the priority security line and then in the direction of the first-class lounge. First class. They were flying first class. Of course they were.

She'd never been in a first-class lounge before. It was luxurious and open, but bright and friendly with decadent décor and dramatic lighting. The seats were comfortable and the service impeccable.

But the lounge had a mezzanine level with views across the airport. If she was sitting down, the bottom half of the glass was smoked. But when she stood up... she could see all the planes sitting at their gates, with others taxiing to and from the runways.

Which was why her heart was currently in her mouth. She took another gulp of the champagne that was sitting next to her.

It was ridiculous. It was irrational. And she knew all that.

Over the course of her life she'd been on dozens of flights. But ever since Jason had died, just the glimpse of a plane made her uncomfortable.

Right now, her skin was itching, her breath catching somewhere in her throat and her heart racing inside her chest.

She stood up and made a grab for her bag. "Excuse me."

With her head fixed firmly on the wall adorned with bright prints she made her way to the ladies' room.

The bright lights and white tiles were a relief. Phoebe splashed some water on her face and took some deep breaths. They'd be due to board any minute now. She fumbled in her bag.

Phoebe stared at the pills in her hand. She'd never taken anything like this before.

Never had to. Never wanted to.

But, after verging on a panic attack at the thought of boarding a plane, she'd gone to see her doctor first thing in the morning. She'd been sympathetic, and talked Phoebe through all the irrational fears she had. She'd wanted to try other methods, other therapies, but Phoebe had told her the urgency of the trip and how much depended on it.

So, she'd given her some breathing exercises. A few methods of control, and, as a last resort, the chance to take something that could reduce her anxiety.

There was nothing shameful in taking a few tablets. Lots of people had problems flying. Once the flight had taken off, she could try and sleep. And once they were due to land again, she could take another.

It was a temporary measure. She looked at her own reflection in the mirror. Life with Jason had been easy, relaxed. He'd been her best friend.

But New Year's Eve with Matteo had been entirely different. The fireworks hadn't just been exploding outside the room. And that connection had been terrifying. Not least, because there seemed to be so much that Matteo was hiding.

She splashed more water. Three years. Three years since Jason was gone. He wouldn't recognize the wide-eyed, terrified girl in the mirror right now. Her hand went to her throat as she held back a sob. And he would hate the fact that she was now petrified of the thing that he loved. The thing that had practically flowed through his veins.

She took a deep breath and shoved the tablets back in her bag. She tried a few of the breathing exercises her doctor had shown her. She could do this. She could do it. She could get on this plane and land in Rome. Yesterday had been key. She'd gone home to the final bill for her mother's medical expenses. She needed this money. She needed to be paid. This job would lift a huge weight off the shoulders of both herself and her mother. The last thing she wanted was for her mother to be stressed about paying for her treatment. Stress could impede her full recovery and Phoebe would never let that happen.

She walked outside. Matteo was pacing outside the door impatiently. "Are you ready? It's time to board."

Phoebe gulped. The sooner this was over—the better.

What was wrong with her? She'd checked her seat belt a dozen times and had her eyes fixed firmly on the screen in front of her. Her endless fidgeting was driving him nuts. Phoebe had never struck him as a fidget.

"Miss? Can I get you a drink prior to departure?" The stewardess had a trolley filled with fine wines, champagnes and spirits. Phoebe glanced in the direction of the trolley for a few seconds, then shook her head. "No. No, thank you."

Her hands twisted in her lap again as the stewardess moved away and a few minutes later the plane started taxiing. Phoebe leaned back in her seat and closed her eyes, her hands gripping the seat rests so tightly her knuckles were white.

A strange feeling washed over Matteo. She'd objected quite strongly to the trip to Rome. "Phoebe, are you scared of flying? Haven't you ever flown before?"

She didn't even open her eyes, or release her grip. There was a tic at the side of her jaw as she spoke through clenched teeth. "I've flown lots of times. Just not recently."

"And are you always like this when you fly?"

He was astonished. She generally seemed quite relaxed and happy. This was a whole other side of her.

The plane started to pick up speed for take-off. As the nose lifted her hand stopped gripping the seat rest and grabbed his hand, squeezing so tightly he lost all feeling in his fingers.

Matteo leaned back in his seat and said nothing. It seemed Phoebe's grip was stronger than expected. After a few minutes he put his other hand over hers. "Phoebe, you okay? Want to talk?"

Now he was feeling guilty. He'd given her an ultimatum. He'd forced her to come on this trip. He'd been so blindsided by getting the houses finished and on the market that he hadn't really considered anything else.

Phoebe started doing some breathing exercises. In. Out. In. Out. He felt himself breathe along with her. Now he knew why she'd been so tetchy. He should have considered something like this.

"Take it easy, Phoebe. We're up. Safe take-off. You can relax."

She opened her eyes, and he was surprised to see they were wet with tears. "I won't relax until we're back on the ground."

"You're *that* scared of flying? Why didn't you say?"

She pressed her lips together and shook her head. "I couldn't. It's new. Well, not that new."

He rubbed her hand again. "At some point I'm going to have to regain the feeling in my fingers. I might need them." He gave her a gentle smile. "What happened that you feel like this?" He knew he was prying. He knew this was none of his business. But he hated seeing Phoebe like this.

Her grip loosened just a little on his hand, but she didn't pull it away. "Sorry," she breathed, then stayed quiet for a few minutes. After a bit she licked her lips and met his gaze. "I had a fiancé. Jason. He was a pilot. He died in a flying accident three years ago."

It was like being punched in the guts. A fiancé?

"I'm sorry, Phoebe. I had no idea." He couldn't help the next words. "What happened?"

She blinked. Her voice was a little shaky. "Engine failure. Double engine failure. Something that shouldn't happen. Jason tried to land the plane. He had to divert it away from a built-up area and ended up crashing in woods." She gave her head a shake. "I've just had a thing about flying since then." She took a deep breath. "I had a funeral to go to last year—an old school friend. I'd bought a plane ticket but just couldn't do it. I ended up driving the four and a half hours to Washington instead of taking the hour-long flight."

"Is this the first flight you've been on?"

She bit her lip and nodded. Matteo hadn't let go of her hand yet. He gave it another squeeze. "You should have told me."

She raised her eyebrows. "I tried to say no. You didn't like that."

He sighed. "I thought you were just reneging on the deal. I didn't know there was something else going on. If you'd told me, I would have acted differently."

"Would you?"

"Of course I would." He waited a few seconds then added, "But I'm really glad you're here. Just wait. It will be worth it. The first time you do anything again is always the hardest."

She frowned as she looked at him, almost as if she were connecting the words with something else, then she gave him a soft smile and nodded. "You could be right."

He leaned over and whispered in her ear. "I promise you, you'll love Rome, and you'll love the house."

"I hope so," she said, as she leaned back in her chair and finally pulled her hand away.

Matteo stared down at his hand.

All of a sudden it surprised him how empty his hand felt.

He glanced sideways. Phoebe had been engaged. She'd had a fiancé.

He couldn't help but be curious about the man that had captured Phoebe Gates's heart.

He just couldn't figure out why it made him so uncomfortable.

The plane gave a jolt and Phoebe felt a tear escape down her cheek. She couldn't breathe. Was it engine failure? What if she never saw her mother again?

Matteo's hand closed over hers again. "Grip as hard as you like. It's just a little bit of turbulence. I can take it." He gave her a reassuring smile. "I'm here with you, Phoebe. We'll get through this."

His green eyes were warm and sincere. She couldn't help the second tear that slid down her cheek. Matteo reached up with his free hand and gently brushed it away. "Tell me about Jason," he said. "Tell me what he was like."

The breath that was caught in the back of her throat came out steadily. "He...he was good," she murmured. "He was great." It was odd to talk about Jason with someone that had never known him. Her brain tried to sort out her jumbled thoughts. "He was a couple of years older than me. We met in Central Park when I was nineteen. He was already in the navy, training as a pilot." She nodded. "He loved his job, completely loved it. Flying was a huge part of his life."

"And you?"

Matteo's finger started tracing soothing circles on the back of her hand. "Oh, he loved me too. Just as much as I loved him." Her voice stuttered a little as a memory swamped her. But it was a good memory, something that made her happy. "He used to make me laugh. He used to make me laugh so hard my sides hurt." She shook her head. "And he shared my sci-fi addiction. Any film, any TV series that was remotely sci-fi was always playing in the background. It didn't matter how bad it was." She smiled. "We watched it anyway."

She was aware of the gentle movements of his finger. She knew he was trying to distract her. Trying to keep her calm. But somehow, in the midst of all this, talking about Jason felt good.

"He'd left the navy and had just got a job as a commercial pilot. We were trying to make plans. Get our lives on track for the future." Her voice drifted off.

Matteo didn't jump in. He didn't push her for more. He just kept doing what he was doing, watching her with those dark green eyes with tiny flecks of gold. "He sounds like a great guy."

She nodded. "He was. And he was big." She shook her head. "We looked like the odd couple." She held up one hand. "I'm not exactly in the tall department and Jason was six foot six." She raised her eyebrows. "It certainly came in handy when I had any clients I felt uncomfortable around. One look from Jason was enough."

The air hostess bumped past them with the drinks trolley. It seemed the turbulence had ended and the "fasten seat belt" sign was off now.

It was nice. It was nice to talk about Jason and remember him. Remember how much she loved him and the part he'd played in her life. "Thank you," she whispered.

"What for?"

She stared down at their hands. "For this. For distracting me. For letting me talk. For letting me remember."

"Don't you talk about Jason?"

She gave him a sad smile. "Sometimes with my mom. But I think she worries it makes me sad. What I worry about is forgetting. I feel guilty."

Matteo pressed his lips together for a second. His voice was husky. "Remembering is good. We'll never be able to remember every detail." He put one hand on his heart, while using the other to intertwine his fingers with hers, "But what we hold in here is really important. Anyone we lose, we carry them with us every day. In our hearts and in our minds. That's what's important."

There was something about the way he said the words that made her heart give a little flip. He understood. He got it.

And all of a sudden so did she. She'd loved Jason for so long. She always would. She shouldn't be scared of forgetting him—that wouldn't happen. But that didn't mean that once she was ready, she wouldn't be able to open her heart to someone else.

She shouldn't feel guilt. Jason would have hated that. She nodded at Matteo as her heart gave another little pitter-patter against her chest.

"You're right," she said quietly. "That's exactly what's important."

The heat levels in Rome were mild. But compared to the chill of New York, it was practically balmy.

After their connection on the plane, Matteo seemed more relaxed in Rome; he spoke his native language fluently and she almost laughed out loud at the gestures he used when chatting to others. In New York, he was so much more reserved.

She was tired. She'd only managed a few hours' sleep on the flight over the Atlantic and the bright morning light of Rome felt harsh on her eyes. But Matteo had assured her that the family home in Rome was much more habitable than the one in the Hamptons, and the interior design work would be much less intense.

The car passed through Rome, giving Phoebe a few glimpses of some of the wonders. She couldn't help but smile. "First time in Rome?" asked Matteo.

"First time in Italy," she breathed. "I've always wanted to come here."

Matteo gave a small nod. "We'll need to try and see if we can fit in some sightseeing."

"Really?" She hadn't expected that from him, and when he gave another nod she settled back into the soft leather seats and took a deep breath. Rome. Wonderful.

The car pulled onto a long winding road set on a hill. After a few minutes a sixteenth-century-style house appeared in front of her with panoramic views over Rome, the sea and Tivoli.

"How beautiful," sighed Phoebe as the driver stopped the car and came around to open the door for her.

Matteo opened the front door to the house and gave her a smile as they stepped onto the red-tiled floor. He waited a few seconds as she let out a gasp.

He gave a nod of acknowledgement. "The villa contains within its walls works of art by masters of the sixteenth and seventeenth centuries. The galleries and lounges all have late baroque and rococo frescoed ceilings. I think you'll like all the features—the oval staircase, the *trompe-l'oeil*, the wood paneling and the parquet."

Even though she was tired from the flight the sight of the magnificent villa was enough to kick-start her again. Matteo did a walk through, showing her the five elegant state rooms and thirteen bedrooms. "This place is wonderful," she said as she clasped her hands to her chest. "Why on earth would your family want to sell it?"

Matteo shrugged and held out his hands. "Because we never use it. You're right. It is a great property, but when anyone from the family is in Italy we are generally down at the villa in Tuscany where the vineyards are. In the last year I think someone from the family had used this villa for less than two weeks. We only stay here for the odd day on business. It doesn't make sense to keep the house any longer."

Phoebe gave a nod. "It just seems such a shame."

Matteo turned back to her. "So, what do you think? Can you can dress this place to sell?"

Phoebe nodded. "Without a doubt. And you're right. It won't take much." She gave a little smile. "Because this has been a family home, it really just needs a little..." she tried to find the right word "...streamlining."

Matteo raised his eyebrows. "You mean decluttering?"

She smiled. "I might. The selling point for this house is actually the frescos. Everything else just needs tailing back to let them shine. And I need to help with the flow of the house. That can be done easily by having one color palette throughout the house. I think cream would work best with a few little splashes of red. That will complement the tiled floor and the frescos."

Matteo nodded. "I think that could work." He slipped his jacket off. "Which room would you like?"

"Excuse me?"

"Which room? You can pick any one you like."

"We're staying here?"

He looked surprised. "I'm sorry. I thought I'd told you that. I imagine you want to get some sleep. Even for a few hours? Then perhaps I can take you to one of the warehouses in Rome. I had my PA search out places similar to the one in New York. I thought it would save some time. Then, we can have a late dinner." He gave a soft smile. "I'm sure we'll be able to find somewhere in Rome no matter what time it is. I know you think New York is the city that never sleeps, but give Rome a chance, I think you'll like it."

She wasn't quite sure what to say. "You seem to have everything planned."

He nodded. "I feel at home here. So, pick a room. Which one did you like best?"

She tilted her head. "Isn't one of these rooms yours?"

He waved his hand. "That doesn't matter. I'm happy to sleep in any of the rooms."

She gave a smile and a small nod. "In that case, I'll take the room at the back that looks out over the garden."

"The one that can give you a glimpse of the Coliseum?" He smiled knowingly.

"And the one with the huge canopy over the bed and the ceiling fan."

He laughed. "It's all yours."

She glanced at her watch. "What time should we get up?"

There was a pause as Matteo met her gaze with an amused expression. Blood rushed to her face. What time should *we* get up? She hadn't meant it like that, but sheer exhaustion was obviously taking its toll.

She shook her head as Matteo put a hand on her shoulder. "I'll get someone to wake you around one p.m. If *we* sleep too late," he emphasized the word with a glint in his eye, "it will knock off our body clocks."

"I guess you're right." She looked around for her bag, but Matteo shook his head. "Don't worry. Carlo, the driver, has taken it up to your room." He paused for a second. "And, Phoebe?"

"Yes?"

He bent down to her ear. His voice was quiet. "Today I think you were exceptionally brave. You should be proud of yourself." He brushed a kiss to the side of her cheek, "Sleep well," he said before disappearing down the corridor.

Phoebe stood in the perfect silence. Outside she could hear the rustle of trees and the chirping of birds. The citrus smell of lemon and orange was drifting through the house.

Maybe it was fatigue, or maybe it was the setting, but Matteo seemed different here. More relaxed. More... accessible.

She put her hands up to her face. The kiss was nothing. A gesture of sympathy. Or maybe of friendship.

She walked up the stairs slowly and crossed into the airy bedroom. The shutters were wide open, allowing her a tiny glimpse of the Coliseum. She smiled. Dressing this house would be a joy and a pleasure.

And maybe something else...

He'd wanted to kiss her. First, on the plane when she'd been so upset. But that had hardly seemed appropriate when she'd mentioned the loss of her fiancé. Then second, when her eyes had lit up with pure pleasure at the house.

Her excitement was palpable. And it felt infectious. No matter how worried he was, no matter how many other things he had on his mind, being around Phoebe just seemed to make the world feel a little more right.

She'd been in the villa five minutes before she'd been able to visualize what she could do to make some improvements. And she'd been right. He'd known that instantly.

A few hours later he was showered, changed and only slightly jet-lagged. Phoebe appeared a little more tired. Dressed in a bright pink dress with a light cardigan, her bag on her arm and a notepad in her hand, she seemed ready to go.

"Would you like to have some brunch?" he asked.

She shook her head and put her hand on her stomach. "I'm feeling a little queasy to be honest. Give my body time to realize what zone it's in." She pulled a bottle of water from her bag. "I'll just stick to this for now." Then she glanced around. "Oh, I'm sorry, you're much more used to traveling than I am. Do you want to have brunch?"

Her openness was so refreshing and his heart gave a little twist. Brave. That was what else Phoebe was. But it wasn't her most obvious trait until you got to know her. Was that what had happened to him? He'd got to know her?

Phoebe had shared probably the worst thing that had ever happened to her. She'd also showed him that fears could be conquered if you really faced up to them.

He could learn a lot from Ms. Gates. He still hadn't had that conversation with Brianna. Every day, time grew shorter. His sister had experienced enough during this pregnancy; at the end she was hoping and praying for a healthy baby—and so was he. But he was also hoping for a happy, healthy sister.

Brianna had no idea what had happened to their mother. She couldn't possibly understand that the happy, well-balanced woman had acted strangely after the delivery of her third child. Matteo hadn't understood it himself. He just remembered her shouting and acting irrationally. But those memories were fuzzy. Because his father had tried to shield him from the worst of it.

As an adult he understood a lot more. Postpartum psychosis had been a little-known diagnosis thirty years ago. His mother had no history of mental health problems. So, her disintegrating mental capacity had bewildered those around her. The sudden paranoia, delusions, severe confusion and manic behavior had been confusing for her friends and family. The ultimate tragic outcome, overdosing on medication and leaving a suicide note, telling her husband how she couldn't bear the thoughts she was having—thoughts of harming her new baby—was quietly hushed up. It was years before Matteo finally put the fragments of his memories together in his brain, and when he had, his father had begged him not to tell anyone else.

But he should tell someone else. He should tell Brianna. Because Brianna was more at risk. Postpartum psychosis could run in families. And from the day and hour his sister had told him she was pregnant, he'd thought about nothing else.

"Matteo?" Phoebe was standing directly underneath him, her hand touching his wrist and her light floral scent floating up around him. Her dark eyes were fixed on his. "Matteo, are you okay?"

He nodded and gave himself a shake. Focus. That

was what he needed to do. "Sure. Everything's fine. Are you ready to see Italian-style warehouses?" He crooked his elbow toward her and she gave a smile as she slid her hand into place.

"Lead the way. I can't wait."

It seemed that Italian warehouses were very like the ones in New York. A few hours of serious shopping seemed to get her most of the things she would need to dress the gorgeous home. By the time they'd finished, the sun was a little lower in the sky and the air a little closer. Matteo made arrangements to get all the goods shipped directly to the villa.

Rome was a bustling, vibrant city. She was here to do a job, but part of her wanted to steal away on one of the open-topped buses to see the sights of the city. What chance would she ever have to come back here?

Phoebe licked her lips and looked around. She'd got on a plane. She'd actually *got* on a plane. And in a few days, she'd have to do it all again. Part of that made her stomach flip-flop. And part of that made her proud. Jason would have been proud of her. Her mother was proud of her. And, she was proud of herself. Even if she was still a little terrified.

It seemed that in the last few weeks she'd made more progress than she had in the last three years. Her first kiss. Her first connection. Her first plane ride. And the one constant thing was Matteo Bianchi.

He turned toward her. "I know you're probably tired, but it's best if we try and stay up late, to try and get into the time zone. How about some dinner and some sightseeing?"

Phoebe raised her eyebrows. "You're actually going to let me see a little of Rome?"

He leaned down and whispered in her ear. "Only the most important parts."

A little tremble snuck down her spine. "Am I dressed appropriately?"

His smile reached from ear to ear. "Oh, don't worry. You're perfect."

When the car pulled up outside the Coliseum bathed in the oranges and reds of the setting sun, Phoebe almost couldn't breathe. She twisted in her chair in excitement. "Is it still open? Can we still go in?"

Matteo gave a nod as the car door opened. "Oh, we can do more than that."

The ancient monument towered above her. Matteo walked around the car and held his hand out toward her. She couldn't help but stare up in wonder as she slid her hand into his. Tingles shot up her arm as Matteo pulled her toward him and slipped his arm around her waist. He held his other hand up to the magnificent structure. "Some of the outer wall has crumbled, due to earthquakes and stone robbers. What you see now is mainly the old interior wall."

Phoebe held her hands in front of her chest. "It's just huge. You can't really understand the size until you're standing right here."

Matteo was still smiling at her. "Can you imagine what this was like? Eighty thousand people crammed in here, shouting, watching the main event—watching the gladiators?"

His words sent a thrill down her spine. There were other people around, late tourists who looked as if they were heading home for the night.

"Can we really go inside?"

Matteo's gaze connected with hers. "Let me give you a special tour. Then we can have dinner."

She stared at him for a few seconds then nodded with excitement. Matteo led her to a special entrance and she held her breath as she walked inside.

There were only a few people left inside the structure. The illumination from the setting sun was a perfect backdrop of orange with streaks of lilac. Phoebe took a few tentative steps forward.

Matteo held out his hands. "Most of the arena floor is gone now—as is a lot of the seating. It was arranged strictly by social status." He raised his eyebrows, "Boxes at the North and South ends for the Emperor and the Vestal Virgins, podiums at the same level for the senatorial class." He gave a little wink. "They could bring their own chairs, you know."

Phoebe let out a laugh. "Really?"

"Really." He pointed to the next row up, "This was for the non-senators or knights, the one above that was for ordinary Roman citizens, split into two parts, one for the rich and one for the poor."

Phoebe gave a nod as she glanced around in wonder. "Hundreds of years on, and we're still obsessed with social class. You'd think we'd be past all that now."

Matteo looked at her thoughtfully. "I know. We should be." They moved a little further into the amphitheater. He pointed out some other parts. "There were specific sections for other people. Boys with their tutors, scribes, priests, soldiers on leave and foreign dignitaries."

"Where did the women get to sit, then?" asked Phoebe. "The ones who *weren't* vestal virgins."

Matteo shook his head. "You might guess. The other

women were allowed to stand with the slaves or the common poor."

Phoebe gave a nod and kept looking around. "Well, I love the wonder of the place. I love the structure. The architecture." She spun around, holding her hands out. "But I'm not sure that I agree with the history of the place."

Matteo held out his hand again. "Come on, I'll show you some more history."

His hand held hers firmly as he led her down some steps. It was darker down here, with some dim lights that only added to the mysterious atmosphere. He gave her a knowing smile over his shoulder. It was colder down here. Threatening. But the warmth from his hand was reaching up all the way to her heart. This was a wonderful surprise. Something she could only have dreamed of. Matteo had done this for her?

He lowered his voice as they walked slowly. "This is the hypogeum. It literally means underground. Two levels with a subterranean network of tunnels and cages underneath the arena where the animals and gladiators were held."

Phoebe stopped walking. "That makes the gladiators sounds like prisoners. I thought the Romans treated them like heroes?"

Matteo pulled a face. "It was complicated. There was a gladiator training school, *ludus magnus,* just outside the Coliseum. The gladiators could come straight through the tunnels to get here. They didn't need to walk with the crowds. Some were volunteers, and some were slaves. Stories about them fighting for their freedom are greatly exaggerated."

Phoebe looked around and rubbed one hand over her arm. All of a sudden this beautiful place gave her chills.

"You okay?"

She gave a small smile. "Maybe just a little over-whelmed. People died here. For sport. I know it's glorified, but suddenly it all seems so real."

Matteo nodded and slipped his arm around her shoulders. "Let's go back upstairs." His arm felt entirely natural there. More than comfortable. It certainly wasn't comfort that was flooding through her veins right now.

He took her up a few flights of stone stairs and walked her out to one of the upper levels. There, sitting in front of her, was a table covered in a white linen cloth with candles flickering on top of it.

It was as if the world stopped.

"What...?"

Matteo walked over and pulled out a chair. "Have a seat, Phoebe. We can look over the rest of Rome as we dine."

She blinked, wondering if any second she was actually going to wake up. "Wh...when you said we were going for dinner I imagined we were going to a restaurant somewhere." She looked around again, not quite believing what she was seeing. The sky had darkened around them, and yellow lights were illuminating the arches of the Coliseum. "I didn't think we would be eating dinner..." she waved her hands "...here."

For a second Matteo looked worried. "You want to eat somewhere else?"

She shook her head as she strode over. "No. Of course I don't." She sat down quickly and a few seconds later her glass was filled with wine and an entrée salad appeared in front of her.

She looked around once again. There was a waiter. But she couldn't see another single person.

"Where is everyone?" she whispered.

"Oh," said Matteo easily, "we have the place to ourselves. The evening tours have just finished and the Coliseum has closed its door to the public."

Phoebe lifted her fork and took a breath. "Matteo, just how rich are you?"

He winked at her. "Not rich at all. Haven't you heard? I'm selling two houses."

She let out a laugh and tried her food. "Did you get them to build a whole kitchen for you too?"

He held up his hands. "You got me. I sweet-talked a local chef at my favorite restaurant."

Now she put down her fork. "You sweet-talked someone? You? Matteo Bianchi? You actually know how to sweet-talk?"

He gave an embarrassed shrug. "Sometimes, I can be nice."

She kept a hint of teasing in her voice. "Just not to me."

He looked at her warily. "I might have been…short with you. But that's all. You think I haven't been nice to you?"

She could see the hint of worry in his eyes. She held out her hands. "Matteo, we're sitting in the Coliseum, in Rome, having a private dinner." She picked up her wine glass and gave an appreciative nod. "I think we can put this one in the nice column."

He sighed as he picked up his wine glass too. "Well, thank goodness. I don't know if we could have made it to the Leaning Tower in time for dessert."

She smiled and leaned across the table toward him, clinking her glass against his. "Hmm… Pisa, now there's a thought."

"You want to visit Pisa too?"

She shook her head. "Not right now. In my lifetime?

Yes, I'd love to. But right now, I'm just getting over the shock of finally getting back on a plane and completing a journey." She picked a little at her salad. "You know, it wasn't quite as bad as I thought."

"No?"

She leaned back in her chair as she studied the beautiful surroundings. "No, it wasn't. It was more just the *thought* of it. All the fears. The expectations. I knew they were irrational. The sensible part of my brain could tell me that." She met his dark gaze and gave him a smile. "I just had problems listening to it." She tilted her head to the side. "I'm not promising I won't be terrified on the way home."

He held her gaze. The candles flickered on the table between them, his dark hair falling across his brow. Her hand itched to reach over and brush it away. To touch him, to feel his skin under the palm of her hand. For a few seconds it really felt as if no one else were there but them.

His voice broke through the silence. It gave the slightest waver. "Sometimes the thought of something is always worse." He bowed his head a little. "And don't be afraid, Phoebe. I'll be with you on the way home."

She could hear the emotion in his voice. His shoulders had tensed, as had his jaw.

"What are you afraid of, Matteo?" The words came out before she could think them through. From the moment she'd met him there had been glimpses of the man struggling to fight his way out from the dark looming cloud that seemed to hang above his head. He was someone in pain—and she could recognize that. She just didn't know if she could help.

She reached across the table and gently interlinked his fingers with hers.

His gaze was dark, intense, but she held it, not letting herself flicker for a second.

"I'm afraid of what might happen to my sister."

"Your sister?"

There was a flash of regret on his face and she could sense his fingers pull away a little. But she held them firmly.

"She's pregnant, isn't she? Why could something happen to her?"

His eyes fixed on the table. He sucked in a deep breath. "Because it happened to my mother."

It was as if the almost mild air in Rome vanished and a chill swept over her body. Every tiny little hair on Phoebe's arms stood on end. Her stomach clenched.

She reached over and put her other hand over their intertwined ones. "What happened to your mother, Matteo?"

He pulled his hand back sharply, throwing it in the air in exasperation as he shook his head. "It's...it's too complicated."

Phoebe nodded her head slowly. "Okay, but..." she glanced around the virtually empty Coliseum "...I think we have time."

She was right at the edge. Dangling. Just waiting to find out what it was that caused Matteo to have that permanent frown marring his complexion. The thing that meant he wasn't quite living life the way he wanted to.

But the moment was broken as the waiter came to lift their plates, and deliver their main course. The rich aroma of ravioli drifted up around her. She stared down at the plate and licked her lips. "Well, it looks delicious. But we're not starting until we finish this conversation."

"It's maybe a good time to have a break," Matteo said quickly as he picked up his fork.

"Stop it," she said sharply, annoyed by how instantly dismissive he could be. She could almost see him putting all his shutters back into place.

"What are you afraid of, Matteo?" She let her voice soften. "Tell me what happened to your mother."

Silence. She didn't fill it. She let him take his time and think. After a few minutes he put his fork down and sighed.

"My mother...my mother committed suicide."

"Oh." Phoebe couldn't help it, her hand had instantly gone to her mouth. "I am so sorry, Matteo, for you and for your brother and sister."

She could see his tongue digging into the side of his cheek. It was clear there was more.

He shook his head again. "My mother...was sick. But the condition she had wasn't well known. Nowadays they would call it postpartum psychosis."

Phoebe wrinkled her nose. She'd heard the expression somewhere but she wasn't quite sure what it was.

Matteo pressed his hands on the table. "My mother didn't have existing mental health problems. But after the birth of my sister—only a few days really—she became confused and a bit manic. I was the oldest, but I was only five. I couldn't really understand what was going on. To be honest, my father didn't understand either. Apparently, it's really rare. It causes depression, paranoia and can cause suicidal thoughts." He took another deep breath. "It can happen in a few days, or a few weeks after delivery of the baby and the onset is really sudden. My mother...she became unwell really quickly. One minute she was walking about the house, talking constantly. Next, she was lying in her bed sobbing. Some nights she didn't sleep, but spent all night pacing the house. My father thought she was just overwrought. But she knew it was more. She knew she was unwell." He wrinkled the fine linen tablecloth in his hands. "Apparently she started to have thoughts about harming my sister. She couldn't make sense of them. She was worried she was going to do something awful. She panicked. She felt as if no one was listening to her—no one really understood how sick she felt. She became absolutely sure she was going to do something to Brianna. She didn't even want to be in the same room as her. So she overdosed."

Phoebe had been leaning back in her chair, trying to comprehend the words that Matteo was saying to her. But as soon as he got to the end of the last sentence she was on her feet instantly, walking around the table and putting her arms around his neck. She didn't hesitate. She sat in his lap and put her forehead against his as the tears welled in her eyes.

"Oh, your poor mother. I can't even imagine how frightened she was." She put her hand on Matteo's chest. His shirt was open at the neck and she could feel his warm skin beneath her fingertips. "And you, as a little boy, must have been terrified by it all."

He gulped. His eyelids were heavy as he lifted his dark eyes to meet hers. She didn't think she'd ever seen such sorrow before. "I found her," he croaked. "She was lying on her bed, with a few of the tablets scattered on the floor. I just thought she was sleeping and I… I was happy, because she'd been so upset before and she looked peaceful. The note was lying on the bedside table but I couldn't read it. It wasn't until I told the housekeeper that she was sleeping, but hadn't woken up for Brianna, that everything seemed to go mad." A single tear slid down his cheek. "I should have told them sooner. I should have known something was wrong."

"No," she said quickly. "You were five. You were a child. You couldn't possibly know or understand." She pressed her head against his. "Oh, Matteo," she breathed as she put a hand at either side of his face. "And you've had this on your shoulders ever since?"

He blinked, with the briefest nod of his head.

"Your brother and sister, they don't know?"

His breathing was a little stuttered. "They know my mother committed suicide." He shook his head. "They don't know the circumstances. My father was never able to talk about it. I found out the real truth much later. I tracked down the housekeeper when I was an adult. She told me exactly how my mother had been in the few days before. She'd ranted to Rosa about wanting to hurt the baby—Brianna. She'd told Rosa to take the baby away from her. She'd been sobbing—breaking her heart. Years on, it's easier to see what happened. But at the time? Any mental health condition was virtually not discussed."

Phoebe wiped the tear away with her finger. "What about Brianna? Why are you worried for her?"

He closed his eyes for a second. She could feel his whole body tremble. "Because it can run in families. If someone else in the family has had it..." His voice tailed off.

Phoebe felt her heart twist in her chest. "You have to tell her. You have to speak to her. You've been carrying this for too long. Your brother and sister are adults. They have a right to know what really happened."

He shook his head fiercely. "I can't tell her. Her pregnancy has been difficult. I can't tell her anything that would put her under stress. This baby means the world to her. They've had problems controlling her blood pressure. They've already told her they might need to deliver her in a few weeks. I can't do anything that would put her blood pressure up and put her, and her baby, at risk."

Phoebe pressed her lips together for a second. "How long? How long have you kept this secret? You're adults, Matteo. You, your brother and sister are all adults. You should have sat down and discussed this a long time ago." She knew it seemed harsh when he'd just bared his soul to her, but she was struggling to get her head around all this. Struggling to understand why the man she'd grown to care about—the man who'd made her start to *feel* again—would have let himself get in this position.

"It's family," he said without hesitation. "You'd do anything for family."

Something started to unfurl deep inside her. She got it. She did. More than he knew.

She kept her voice steady. "Yes. Yes, you would. I understand—probably better than you know."

His expression changed. "What do you mean?"

She licked her lips. "I mean that, for the last six months I've been supporting my mother go through cancer treatment. She's had surgery, radiotherapy and chemotherapy. Part of the reason I took this job was the pay scale. We have huge medical bills to cover. This money…it will make things easier for us. I don't want my mom to have to worry about covering the bills the insurance company won't. She's spent her life, and particularly the last few years, looking after me. It's time for me to return the favor." She met his gaze steadily. "That's why I got on the plane."

"For your mom?" All of a sudden his accent seemed so much thicker.

She nodded. Her insides were twisting. Part of her could tell he might have hoped she'd got on the plane for him. Not for the job. Or for the prestige of working on the house. Or for the chance to visit Rome.

She lifted her hand and paused it for the briefest of seconds before running it through his hair. "I get why you did this, Matteo. But things have changed. You're not a little boy anymore. The world has changed. Diagnosis and mental health services are so much better now. Isn't the way to protect your sister to tell her the truth?"

He held her gaze for the longest of times, as if he was contemplating her words. "It's just never been the right time. Vittore was getting married—then he wasn't. My father got sick. Then we had the funeral. Then there was all the family business to sort out. The houses were the last thing, but then Brianna announced she was pregnant and started having problems—what kind of brother would I be to sit her down and tell her something devastating now?" His hand reached up and closed over hers. He tilted his head to the side and gave her a sorrowful expression. "Why didn't you tell me your mother was sick? Is she okay now? Is she feeling better?"

Phoebe gave a nod. "She's well on the road to recovery with a big support system. I would never have left her if I wasn't sure she was okay." His hand reached up and stroked her cheek.

"But you did," he whispered.

"I did," she replied.

She felt it. The flicker low, deep down in her belly. The tiny pulses emanating out throughout her body. His lips touching hers confirmed everything she needed to know.

Her breath caught in her throat and her eyes filled with tears. Finally, she could acknowledge how she was feeling.

She was ready. She was ready to let go and move on. And she'd found the person she wanted to move on with.

She didn't care that he was her boss. She didn't care they had a million other things to talk about. He needed her just as much as she needed him. There was a reason they'd met.

Matteo Bianchi was her reason to move on. Her reason to let her heart be exposed to the world again.

As that thought crowded her brain she pulled her lips back from his to catch her breath.

She let out a gentle laugh as the scent of the spicy ravioli drifted around them. "I'm sorry," she whispered. "You've gone to such a fabulous effort, and it might smell wonderful, but all of a sudden I'm not so sure I want dinner."

His dark green eyes met hers. This time they were different. There wasn't so much sorrow. This time there was a glimmer of something else. His fingers brushed over her cheek. "I ordered my favorite, but I'm happy to leave it behind."

His hands went to her waist as he eased her from his lap, stood up, then pulled her against him. "How about we go someplace else?" He gave her a sexy smile. "They say the world is your oyster. But tonight—Rome is your oyster. Where would you like to go?"

She slid her arms up around his neck. She was delighting in feeling his body against hers. The angled planes, wide chest and taut muscles. It was easy. It was so easy. And she'd never wanted it more. She put her lips to his ear. "How about we just go home?"

# CHAPTER SEVEN

HE WOKE UP to caramel-colored limbs tangled around his own, and tight springy curls just under his nose. Their breathing was synched. Phoebe's chest rose and fell with his own. The remnants of last night's passion was evident throughout the room. Her shoes were near the doorway. Her pink dress on the wooden floor, close to his pale blue shirt. His trousers were crumpled near the bottom of the bed. As for their underwear? He had no idea what had happened to it.

For the first time in thirty-five years Matteo finally felt a true connection to someone outside his family. He'd had no idea about Phoebe's mom. A tiny selfish part of him had been initially disappointed that she hadn't braved the plane journey for him—but that was ridiculous. Phoebe Gates was the bravest woman he'd ever met. She'd lost her fiancé, helped her mother fight cancer, then faced her biggest fear to complete a job. And the job wouldn't be completed for over a week. Somehow he knew that in that space of time Phoebe could work her magic and sprinkle her fairy dust on this villa. Right now, he was contemplating how many excuses he could make for work that would allow him to stay here this week in Rome with Phoebe.

He hadn't had a vacation in…how long? Plus, he

could fly up and down to some of the vineyards in Tuscany in one day. He could have breakfast with Phoebe in Rome, leave her to do her work while he completed his, then meet her for dinner at night back in Rome. And then...

Something squeezed inside him. Today felt different. Today was the morning after the night before.

The first time he'd shared the secret he'd kept since he was five years old.

For years he'd been haunted by the sight of his beautiful sleeping mother. Thankful she looked so peaceful after a strange few days. Except she hadn't been sleeping. As a child, he would never have known that. Should never have known that. And he'd actually sat on the floor of her room for a while, playing with his trains while Brianna gurgled in the cradle.

It was only when Brianna had started to get noisier and his mother hadn't roused that he'd gone to find someone else. At five, he wasn't quite sure he wanted to pick up the squirming bundle. But he certainly hadn't been ready for the reaction that had followed.

Those days all blurred into one. Police cars. A quietly spoken doctor. People dressed in black around his father. A funeral that he'd never been told about and certainly not been part of. The invasion of a million Italian relatives who all squeezed him tight and whispered to his father. As for the house at the Hamptons? It had more or less been left exactly as they'd found it. They'd been whisked away to the apartment near Central Park where two female relatives of his father had helped settle him and his brother and sister, before hiring help for the new apartment.

But that horrible feeling of something being really wrong had never left him. As a child he'd learned quickly not to ask his father anything about his mother—it just seemed to leave him eternally sad.

As an adult, he'd made a few enquiries. It hadn't been easy. But even when he knew the truth his father had still been pained to talk about it. He'd told Matteo to remember his mother as before, not in her last few days, and not to mention it to his brother or sister.

And Matteo, being the good Italian son that he was, respected his father's wishes.

Suicide. The one subject most people didn't want to discuss. Phoebe's face had crumpled last night. But the one thing that had struck him completely was her empathy. Empathy for the confusion his mother must have been feeling.

But that didn't surprise him. Not at all. On every occasion, Phoebe had proved to him what a good person she was.

But was he as good a person as Phoebe was? Something was unsettling him. Phoebe had been brilliant last night. But there was more. She was blossoming. Phoebe had always had an internal glow—but when he'd first met her it had been tempered.

Yet ever since they'd touched down in Rome, the sparkle in her eyes and passionate nature had been brimming over.

Something twisted inside. Should he really be doing this? He'd never felt a connection like this. He'd never let himself. What if he wasn't enough for Phoebe? The last thing he'd ever want to do was dim the light in the vibrant, happy person she'd become. He was so used to keeping secrets. So used to keeping his emotions in check. Could he ever behave any differently?

And while he was comfortable here, lying with her in his arms, she'd made him face up to his next reality. At some point, he would have to speak to Vittore and Brianna. Just not right now. When Brianna had the baby he would make sure he was around her constantly. He would watch. He would monitor. He'd made a few casual enquiries about what to do if he needed to find some professional help. He was confident, in this day and age, things would be fine. And once that stage had passed, once Brianna had her healthy baby and was settled, he could wait and tell them both at a later date. Things would be fine.

"Hey..." came a murmur.

He glanced down. Phoebe was rubbing her brown eyes; she gave him a sleep-filled smile. "Hey," he replied.

Her stomach gave an involuntary grumble and she let out a deep laugh as she pulled her body back from his and flopped back next to him. Her eyes were twinkling as she turned to him. "I guess this is what happens when you cheat me out of my Italian ravioli."

"*I* cheated you out of your Italian ravioli?" He leaned his head on one hand so he could get closer to her.

Her smile spread from ear to ear. She looked relaxed. She looked *happy*. Something struck him. This was the first time he'd seen her like this. It was almost as if a weight had been lifted off her shoulders. It was something about her eyes. A different kind of shine.

He was getting to see the true heart of Phoebe.

She winked at him. "I also missed dessert." Her hand snaked up around his neck again as she leaned in. "I kind of think that's your fault too. How do you plan on making it up to me?"

He laughed as his hand slid along her silky skin. This felt perfect. It felt so right. If only he could stay just here. If only he could freeze time and let things stay like this. Not have to think about anything else.

Planet Phoebe. No worrying about family. No worrying about business. No selling houses. Just spending the rest of his time with a warm, beautiful, good-spirited woman.

Her stomach growled again. She flipped him onto his back and swung her leg over his body, leaning above him. "Enough, Mr. Bianchi. I think it's time you introduced me to what Italians have for breakfast."

He raised his eyebrows. "Well…when you put it like that…"

She lifted her finger to wag it at him but he spun her onto her back so quickly the breath left her body.

He winked at her. "Let me show you."


The day couldn't be better. Last night had been beautiful, surprising, and then emotional, tense and unbelievably hot.

Every time she closed her eyes she could still feel Matteo's breath on her skin, feel his lips trailing across hers and feel his beating heart next to hers.

The connection was so strong. It was as if now she'd finally decided she was ready to move on, her body and brain had decided to catch up on three years and move at breakneck speed. And although she had the odd thought of caution, Matteo seemed to be matching her every step of the way.

Today had been magical. Matteo had shown her the sights in Rome. He'd taken her to the Sistine Chapel, the Vatican and St Peter's Basilica. Instead of going by chauffeur-driven car, they'd joined the tourists and Phoebe had loved it.

She'd got to see the excitement and wonder on everyone else's faces—just like her own—all the while having Matteo's rich Italian voice in her ear giving her insight and information like her own personal tour guide.

As they lunched at a little restaurant near the Vatican Matteo's phone rang. He finished the call quickly with a huge smile on his face.

She leaned across the table toward him. "What? What is it?"

He shrugged and held up his hands. "It seems that word has got out. The villa isn't even on the market, and yet, my solicitor has just had a very substantial offer on the property subject to a viewing next week."

"Really?" Phoebe could hardly believe it.

"Do you think you can have the house ready for next week?"

She nodded her head. "Of course I can. No problem at all." She raised her glass of wine toward him. "It just goes to show you, someone has probably had their eye on your family villa for years, and has just been waiting for word that you were ready to sell."

Matteo nodded. "It seems likely, and, to be honest, I'm glad. I want the house to be lived in, to be enjoyed the way it should be. I've always hated the fact that the villa has virtually been unused for the last ten years. It should be brought back to life." He lifted his wine glass to Phoebe. "It seems you might just be my good luck charm."

Her heart gave a little flutter. She clinked her glass against his. "Maybe I am. I guess we just need to find out."

The smile he gave her in return sent little shivers of expectation down her spine and they spent the rest of the afternoon drinking wine and coffee, then finishing with the most wonderful tiramisu. Matteo held her hand across the table the whole time, listening to her ideas for the villa with interest. But when he started talking about plans for them going home her expression must have changed.

"Phoebe, are you okay?"

She nodded nervously. One mention of going home made her mouth go dry. She'd made it on the plane out here. Of course she knew she'd have to make the same journey as before. But last time around, there wasn't so much time to think about it. Matteo had booked the flights, she'd visited her doctor and felt as if there was a push to come here. The whole chance of not being paid had huge implications for her; it was the biggest motivator for getting on that plane.

But for the journey home?

Matteo now knew about her mother. He wouldn't withhold payment. Yes, she would complete the job in Rome, but right now the thought of getting on another plane was making her want to be sick.

She gave Matteo a weak smile. "I'm just trying not to think about the flight home. I know it's more than a few days away. But I guess one flight isn't enough to cure my fear. I'm worried I'll be like this forever. Spending my whole life wanting to be sick all over my shoes and having palpitations at the mere thought of a flight."

Matteo put his other hand over the top of hers and squeezed. "But I'll be with you. I'll be with you every step of the way. Don't worry. And this time, you'll have my full attention. You don't need to worry." He gave her a wicked smile. "I have lots of ways to distract you—if you'll let me. Or, I can just hold your hand. And you can squeeze mine until there's no blood flow and it's a strange shade of purple. Whatever you like."

She took a deep breath and smiled. She would always

be nervous. She didn't imagine those feelings would ever go away. But having someone who would support her would make things a little easier. Someone she could rely on. Someone she could trust.

It swept over her. Like a warm, soothing breeze. Someone she might love.

For the tiniest second she couldn't breathe. It felt as if a little flower were blooming and opening in her chest. She'd had her heart sealed off and protected for so long—she'd just never thought she would get here again.

And now, when she least expected it, Matteo had just bolted into her life. With his brisk, businesslike manner she hadn't expected to be attracted to him. But somehow or other, this man with so many barriers in place, yet with a rich sexy accent and the occasional cheeky twinkle in his eye, had made her feel a whole lot of something.

Sometimes love caught you unawares.

She reached her other hand over Matteo's. "I think I might like that." She smiled. They stayed like that for a few minutes, their gazes meshed, just touching, against the backdrop of St Peter's Basilica—one of the most beautiful places in the world. Life really couldn't be more perfect.

She'd told him her biggest secrets, and he'd told her his. But together they could do this. He would support her. And she would support him with what he needed to do when he got home.

Matteo reached over and gently stroked the side of her face. "Thank you for being here," he whispered. "I can't imagine being here with anyone else. Just you, Phoebe. You make Rome perfect for me."

Her heart swelled in her chest. He felt the same as she did. So she did what felt entirely natural. She leaned forward and met his lips with hers. "You do the same for me."

Nothing felt so sweet. Nothing felt so right. She would remember this moment forever.

When they finally pulled apart, Matteo laughed and straightened his clothes. "I guess we should take a walk. I think I might need to cool off a little."

Strolling through Rome with Matteo's arm over her shoulders couldn't have been sweeter.

She should have really spent all day working at the villa in Rome—after all, that was why she was there—but she was confident she would be able to do the task over the next week.

Since they'd arrived back at the villa she'd spent the last hour writing notes for work tomorrow, and then dressed for dinner. Apparently, tonight she would get to taste the best ravioli in Italy.

She tugged at the red dress she was wearing. It was a little longer than she normally wore, but the light floaty fabric skimmed her curves in a way she liked and it would be perfect for dinner.

Matteo was waiting for her downstairs. He met her with a kiss that made her knees tremble and sent little sparks flying around her body.

But as they went to leave Matteo's phone rang.

"I'll switch it off," he said quickly as he pulled it from his pocket. But his brow dipped sharply once he glanced at the screen.

He didn't hesitate to answer. "Brianna?"

Phoebe felt her heart squeeze in her chest. She walked straight over and put her hands on his other arm. "What is it?"

He changed from English and started speaking rapidly in Italian. She could see him trying to stay calm, even though his words were coming out more frantically and more sternly.

She hated the fact she couldn't understand almost as much as she hated the fact she couldn't hear what was being said at the other side. "Is she okay?"

Matteo blanched. His tone of voice changed. She heard his brother's name. Vittore. At that point, he launched into a tirade, before walking over to the house phone and starting to dial another number.

"What can I do? What can I do to help you?"

But Matteo didn't seem to hear her. He moved between phone calls. Hanging up on the mobile and giving rapid instructions—still in Italian—into the house phone.

When he finally hung up he looked as if he'd aged ten years in a few minutes. "What is it?" she persisted.

"Brianna. She went into hospital yesterday and didn't let Vittore tell me. Things are bad. They have to deliver the baby in the next few hours. I have to go home."

Phoebe blinked then nodded. "Absolutely. Of course you do. I'll pack."

"No."

His voice was sharp. It was almost as if he'd switched off and gone into automatic pilot. "You stay here. You finish the house. Make it ready for the viewing next week that will complete the sale. That's what I need you to do right now."

"But your family?" Phoebe took a deep breath. "Maybe you should speak to Vittore before you take off. Let him know you're worried. Tell him why. He'll be with Brianna for the next few hours."

He drew back and looked at her as if she were crazy. "I can't tell Vittore something like that on the phone.

That's ridiculous. I need to be with my family right now. I can't stay here with you."

It was like a chill washing over her body. It wasn't the words. It was the way that he said them. In the last twenty-four hours she'd never felt as connected to someone as she did to Matteo. But he was acting as if the last twenty-four hours hadn't happened—as if they meant nothing at all. Had she been stupid? Had she imagined something that wasn't actually real? Her automatic reaction was to self-protect. To withdraw. "I'm not asking you to. I absolutely understand you going to your sister. I would never ask you not to do that."

She turned around, trying to ignore the pain washing over her body.

She put her hand on the metallic rail of the staircase and held her breath, squeezing her eyes closed for a second, and praying that he might reconsider—praying that he might say something else. Anything to acknowledge the connection between them. Anything that might make her realize this wasn't all one-sided. That he might love her as much as she loved him.

But there was nothing. Matteo completely ignored her. He shouted a few commands in Italian to some of the staff at the villa then stalked off into his study to grab a few items.

A few minutes later the car pulled up in front of the villa, ready to take him straight to the airport. Phoebe hadn't moved much. She'd only made it to the top of the stairs.

There was a fist clenching around her heart. She knew how upset he was. And she got it. She did.

But she also knew that no matter how worried or upset she was about her mother, she wouldn't treat Matteo so dismissively. She would at the very least try and take a few minutes to explain—to let him understand.

But it seemed that Italian men were different. She knew Italians were famous for family loyalty. But she couldn't imagine that Matteo could love his family any more than she did hers.

But, it appeared, it didn't matter. Matteo appeared a few moments later with a bag in hand.

"Matteo?"

He glanced up at her. But the look he gave her was so detached—a world away from the connection of earlier. Her insides felt as though she were on a roller coaster.

His shutters were back in place. The ones he continually hid behind. The ones she'd thought she'd broken through.

He let out a sigh. But it seemed almost dismissive. He shook his head. "It's better this way, Phoebe." He paused then added, "Better for us both." He turned and swept out of the door into the dark night.

It appeared that her plane ride home would be taken alone—the thing that she'd always dreaded.

She couldn't depend on Matteo after all. And why should she?

She was just an employee.

# CHAPTER EIGHT

PHOEBE WORKED ON automatic pilot. It was easy. She'd already made the plans for the house and just saw them through to perfection.

The staff in the villa looked after her well. All of them could speak English and translated anything for her that she required and dealt with any orders or deliveries she needed.

By the end of the week the villa was immaculate and ready for viewing.

And Matteo hadn't called. Not once.

Nor did he call when she contacted the family solicitor to arrange the viewing.

Nor did he call when she arranged her flight home.

Curiosity was killing her. Her fingers found the Hampton house listed for sale on the Internet. The photographs were gorgeous, capturing the true beauty of the surroundings and the stunning views.

And it seemed that word had spread. Her phone hadn't stopped ringing with offers of new jobs. The solicitor in Italy sent her photographs to use from the villa for her portfolio. She updated her website adding the Italian villa and the Hampton house.

She never discussed the flight home with anyone. The first flight she'd actually refused to board, frozen to her seat in the departure lounge, trying to remember all her breathing exercises.

Thankfully for her, one of the airline staff had taken pity on her. Marsha had experienced many nervous flyers and had been due to fly home herself. She'd distracted Phoebe before the next flight, and held her hand through the take-off and the landing. Laughing off the fact that Phoebe must have practically crushed every bone in her hand.

And after she'd returned, nothing. Not a word. Not a single word from Matteo.

"You tell us this now?"

Vittore was furious, and didn't care who knew about it.

Brianna seemed calmer. She walked over to the bassinet and laid Jay down with barely a flicker of emotion. It was only as she moved back over toward Matteo, taking his arm and steering him sharply out of the room, did he see the little flicker at her jaw. She gestured with her head for Vittore to follow, before closing the doors firmly behind her.

"What?" was her only response.

Matteo licked his dry lips. "I'm sorry," he said simply. "I wanted to tell you both before. But...it didn't seem appropriate."

Vittore was in his face in an instant. "In thirty years—you couldn't find an appropriate time? We've spent our whole lives together, Matt. This was the first time you thought to tell us?" His face was scarlet and his hands were in fists at the sides of his body.

"Of course it wasn't! But I haven't known since I was five. I figured it out. Papa would never discuss it. Never. On the few occasions I tried to ask him about it, it was clear I was upsetting him. He always told me to leave it."

"You found her. You never told us that before." Brianna's voice was quiet, but packed with emotion. Vittore turned to their sister, his face wracked with confusion; it was clear he expected her to be angry too.

Matteo sucked in another breath. "Yes." His voice shook. He couldn't help it. "I thought she was sleeping."

Once he'd started telling his brother and sister, things had just spilled out, often in the wrong order. But he couldn't keep it together any longer. He'd spent the last month practically on Brianna's shoulder and it was clear she was suspicious of his overly protective behavior. At first, she'd thought he was just a smitten uncle. But after a few weeks, she'd become more in tune to his observations and questions.

Ever since he'd taken that panicked flight home from Rome he'd felt as if he'd been living on a knife edge. Phoebe's words had constantly echoed in his brain. The last look on her face haunted him.

He tried to persuade himself it was for the best. He'd never be enough for the bright shining star that was Phoebe Gates. Things would cool, fade and be a disappointment for her. Walking away at this point was actually protecting her—saving her from any future pain he might cause.

But the truth was he'd been so focused on his family he hadn't left any room for her. It was a mistake. A massive mistake. And the only person he'd been trying to protect was himself. Protecting himself from actually sharing the love and emotional commitment that came from being in a loving relationship with someone who could potentially hurt him. Just as his mother had.

He'd felt abandoned by his mother. Let down.

Surely if she'd loved him more she wouldn't have committed suicide—wouldn't have left him, Vittore and Brianna?

He'd also felt responsible. If he'd sounded the alarm sooner—maybe something could have been done—maybe his mother's life could have been saved and he wouldn't have grown up with his heart locked away. Scared to let anyone hurt it again.

All thoughts and feelings that any psychologist in the world could pick apart and dissect, and reconstruct in a more healthy, rational manner.

But never had it been clear to him until this moment.

He'd spent the last month tiptoeing around Brianna, watching for any sign of postpartum psychosis. Any sign that might alert him, as an adult, to what he'd missed as a child.

But Brianna was just Brianna. Initially elated and overwhelmed with parenthood like any new mom. Then tired, over-emotional and occasionally irrational. Entirely just Brianna.

But there was something else too. A side he'd never seen of his sister. He was obviously imagining it, but sometimes he could swear Brianna just seemed to glow. Jay had put the biggest smile on his sister's face that he'd ever seen. In fact, Jay had put the biggest smile on the whole family's face. The little guy just had to make one squeak and there were ten adults around the crib, palms itching to pick him up.

Brianna walked across the room and wrapped her arms around her brother. "How long have you felt like this? Have you always felt like this? You thought she was sleeping?" Brianna shook her head as a single tear fell down her cheek. "That's so much for a kid to shoulder. Didn't you have anyone to talk to about it?"

Matteo shook his head. Vittore sat down on the chair next to him. "So...how did you find out? You said you figured it out."

Matteo nodded slowly. "Do you remember Rosa, our housekeeper?"

Both shook their heads.

"Of course you don't. You were both too young. Never mind. I tracked Rosa down. She could fill in all the details. She told me about the note and what was in it. She told me exactly how Mom had been acting— what she'd been saying. Rosa had been so upset about what happened. It turns out in later life she'd been diagnosed herself with depression. Her own psychiatrist and counsellor told her what Mom's likely diagnosis was. Thing were different thirty years ago and it wasn't well recognized or diagnosed. They helped her come to terms with the fact that she hadn't done anything wrong. And she...helped me understand that my mother had committed suicide out of complete desperation. She didn't want to harm her baby. She couldn't stop the way she was feeling, and she couldn't bear feeling like that. She didn't feel as if she could be responsible for her own actions."

Matteo's words hung in the air as Vittore put his head in his hands, and Brianna stared wordlessly at the doors behind which her baby lay.

She put her hand to her chest. "So, the risks, the worry. Why were you worried about me?"

Matteo reached over and clasped her hand. "Because women who have a close relative who've suffered from postpartum psychosis are slightly at higher risk."

"That's why you've spent the last month looking over my shoulder?"

Matteo cringed and nodded.

"You couldn't just tell me?" She held her hands out. "Tell us? Then I could have spoken to my physician. Asked him about the risks. Don't you think that would have made more sense?"

He shook his head slowly. "It might seem that way. But how could I tell you? Your blood pressure was up, you'd had that scare…what kind of brother would I be if I'd told you something like that, at a time when the last thing you needed was stress?"

Brianna gave him a sad smile. "I understand. I do." She looked around and put her hands on his shoulders. "Now I get it. Now I understand why you wanted to sell the Hamptons so quickly. Why you wanted to get rid of the place."

Something washed over him. A realization.

He looked at them both. "You don't?"

Brianna and Vittore exchanged glances. Vittore frowned a little. "Well, obviously it's worth millions of dollars. But I don't have bad memories of the house—to be honest, I don't have any memories at all. I've always thought of it as a bit of a forgotten beauty. I've always been sorry it's been neglected and left empty."

"Do you want it?" Somehow that made Matteo's skin prickle.

Vittore shook his head. "I spend most of my life in California. What would I do with a house in the Hamptons?"

Matteo turned to his sister. "Brianna?"

She shook her head. "I love my place here in the city. I don't want to move to the Hamptons. But I don't care about selling. I never really have. I just went along with it because you seemed so insistent." She waved her hand. "I understand about the villa in Rome. It seemed ridiculous to keep it when we are never there. And your interior designer? Oh, my goodness. What a great job she's done. The photographs are amazing. As for the selling price for the house…"

As Brianna's voice tailed off Matteo sagged in the chair. Every time he'd thought about Phoebe in the last few weeks he'd felt instantly sick. He'd let her down. He'd left her.

He'd known exactly how worried she was about the flight, but he'd been so worried about Brianna he couldn't even think straight. He'd convinced himself he was protecting Phoebe by leaving the way he did. Someone as closed off as him could never offer her the love and life she deserved. As soon as he was back, he'd arranged the transfer of her fee for doing all the work on both houses. The offer for the villa in Rome had been more than expected. It seemed that someone had their eye on the place and was waiting to snap it up.

But who was he kidding? Phoebe might need the money to pay her mother's medical bills but, somehow, he knew that the transfer of the money was a cold, hard way to complete the end of their business.

As for the house in the Hamptons? He'd had three offers already. But something had stopped him discussing them with his brother and sister, and until this minute he hadn't really understood why.

He lifted his head.

Now he was seeing the house through new eyes—eyes like Phoebe's. Because now when he thought of the house at the Hamptons, his first thought wasn't a sad, horrible one of his mother dying. Now his first thought was bright, and featured Phoebe dancing on the stairs in her yellow dress. When he closed his eyes he could see the brilliant light shining through all the windows in the house, leaving it clean and airy. When his mind drifted, it went straight to the red library with a fire burning, a comfortable rug and fireworks going off in the background.

Phoebe had done this. He'd made these memories with Phoebe.

All of a sudden he realized that the heart he'd been guarding so fiercely had a mind of its own.

"Matteo, what's wrong?" Vittore was looking at him curiously.

Matteo ran his fingers through his hair. "I might have done something I shouldn't."

"Again?" Vittore raised his eyebrows.

Matteo stood up and started to pace. "I might have treated someone...not as well as I could have." There was a hideous sinking feeling in his stomach. "I might have made a big mistake."

Brianna's eyes locked onto his. "What did you do?"

The sinking feeling changed to more like a plummet to the bottom of the Marianas Trench. This time there was no "thinking."

"I've made the biggest mistake of my life."

Vittore looked at him in complete confusion. He turned to Brianna. "Do you have any idea what he's talking about?"

Brianna nodded. "Unfortunately, I think I do." She gave a little smile. "And I think her name is Phoebe."

# CHAPTER NINE

IT WAS DARK. She hadn't meant to stay out so late. But she'd been on a date.

A date.

It was a month since she'd seen or heard from Matteo. She hoped and prayed that his sister was well. But after that? She refused to allow him anymore space in her brain.

She'd checked yesterday and the house in the Hamptons still wasn't sold. That surprised her. She was sure it would have sold quicker than this. It made her stomach flip-flop a little. Maybe she hadn't done as good a job as she thought?

Nonetheless, it was time for some changes. Work was flooding in. There had been a sizeable bank transfer into her account and she'd wasted no time in paying her mother's bills. There was no doubt. It was a weight off her mind.

Last week a casual acquaintance had asked her out for dinner. For the last three years her default position had been to automatically refuse. But this time, she hadn't. This time she'd agreed—which had resulted in dinner tonight.

He'd booked an Italian restaurant and it would have been rude to insist on going someplace else. So Phoebe had smiled and tried not to baulk when John, her date, had ordered ravioli. It was almost as if everything about this date was trying to stir up memories of Matteo.

Two glasses of wine later it was clear there was no spark, no electricity—at least on Phoebe's side. And John had been gentlemanly enough to accept her thanks for dinner graciously before she'd made her excuses and left.

Trouble was…the date had stirred up a lot of emotions and as she'd walked home she'd ducked into a little jazz club and sipped a cocktail for an hour, soaking up the music and trying to shake off her melancholy feelings.

She climbed the stairs to her apartment on automatic pilot but when she turned the corner she stopped dead.

Flowers. Lots of them. All lined up outside her apartment door.

Her neighbor, Latisha, must have heard her footsteps because she opened her door and folded her arms across her chest. "Well, Phoebe Gates. What have you been up to?"

Phoebe shook her head as she walked up and down the line.

"These are for me?"

"Do you think I would have left them in the hall if they were for me?"

Phoebe shook her head and bent down and plucked the card from the first beautiful display of yellow roses.

*Can we talk please?*
*Matteo.*

She pulled a face and stopped herself from throwing the card on the floor.

Latisha raised her eyebrows. "Oh, don't worry, honey, I've read all the cards."

Phoebe looked at the line and counted along, "Six, seven, eight, nine."

Latisha smiled. "He gets kind of desperate at the end. Apparently there'll be a car outside for you at nine tomorrow morning."

Phoebe shook her head as she stomped past the coral-colored roses, the white lilies and the purple lisianthus. "I'm not getting in any car."

"Well, honey, if you don't, *I will.*"

Phoebe spun around and glared at Latisha. "You would not."

Latisha looked along the line of flowers on the floor. "I wouldn't? Whatever it is he's done, I guess he's sorry."

"Not sorry enough!" Phoebe slammed her door closed and squeezed her eyes closed for a second, willing the tears away.

He'd left her. He'd left her to fly home alone when he'd known how scared she was. He'd waited more than a month to contact her. Why now?

She was angry with herself. Even though she'd spent all night telling herself she wouldn't, by nine a.m. she'd found herself washed, dressed and sitting in her brand-new green coat at her kitchen table.

When the knock at the door came she gulped as a wave of anger swept over her again. She swung the door open and started as she saw Matteo's driver, Carlo.

He gave her a smile. "Morning, Ms. Gates. Are you ready?"

He held out a caramel latte and a strawberry frosted donut. She blinked. It was a little unexpected. Carlo nodded his head toward the line of flowers along the floor.

"You didn't like them?"

Phoebe pressed her lips together. "Flowers aren't an apology," she muttered.

Carlo nodded in agreement. He waved out his hand. "Are you ready?"

She bit her bottom lip. What was she doing? Was she crazy?

She grabbed her bag and pulled the door closed behind her. "Let's go."

The route was familiar. It didn't take her long to realize where they were going. For a few minutes she had a mild panic. Were they returning to the home in the Hamptons because Matteo's family were unhappy with her work? Surely, if they were unhappy they wouldn't have paid her?

She took a deep breath and settled back against the comfortable leather seat. New York City disappeared behind them making way to the cute streets of the villages and to the wide open spaces of the Hamptons.

By the time they turned into the driveway of the house her stomach was churning.

Carlo pulled up outside and opened the door for her. She waited a few seconds, sucking in a few steadying breaths before she grabbed her bag and stepped out.

She hated it. The way she loved this place. The way just being here made her skin tingle. She knew this place was blackened and tinged with bad memories for Matteo, and maybe now she should have a few bad memories herself. But she couldn't. She just couldn't. Every part of her loved this place. Every room. Every piece of furniture. Every scent. And every thought.

Because most of them were filled with Matteo.

She tried to clear her head. She tried to focus. Flowers, coffee and donuts were not an apology. Not in this lifetime.

She might have decided she was ready to move on. But she would ultimately decide when, and with whom.

Her heels clicked across the marble floor, the steps echoing up the spiral staircase she loved so much. She stopped.

There was a different kind of scent in the house. A mixture of lemon and fresh linen with a hint of something else. Was it lavender?

"Hello?" she shouted. There was no response, so she started to walk. It wasn't as if she didn't know this place.

Flowers. That was the extra scent. Flowers in every room. A different display, sometimes shades of white, yellow and pale blue to match the surroundings. Sometimes something completely different to add a splash of color. As she walked through to the back sitting room, a tall vase of orange gerberas adorned every table.

She walked over and touched one of the petals. Bright orange and green. It was an interesting combination.

There were footsteps behind her. She turned around as Matteo walked in, holding a tray with coffee and a china plate filled with desserts. He gave her a tentative smile. "I visited our favorite bakery and bought you one of everything."

She didn't respond. Just watched as he walked over and slid the tray onto one of the tables.

She was tempted. Tempted by the smells. Tempted by the sight of him again after a month. That strong jaw, his floppy hair and broad shoulders. But she wouldn't waver.

"What is this, Matteo? What do you want?"

It was the first time in her life she'd seen him look a little uncertain.

"I want to talk," he said quietly.

She moved across the floor quickly. "Is something wrong with the house? With my work?"

He shook his head. A familiar furrow creased his brow. "Why would you think that?"

She glanced around. "The house—it's been a month. Why hasn't it sold yet? I know it's the wrong time of year. But a place like this? I expected it to be snapped up in a second."

Matteo licked his lips and nodded. "I've had three offers."

Now it was her turn to wrinkle her brow. "And they didn't offer enough?"

He shook his head and glanced out the window at Mecox Bay. "They offered more than enough. We... I mean... I decided I didn't want to sell."

"You don't?" She couldn't hide the surprise from her voice.

She moved over beside Matteo and hesitated for only a second before sitting down.

He turned to face her. "You made me think about things. You made me think differently—" he held up his hands "—about this place."

She shifted on the seat. "What do you mean?"

He sighed and looked around. "You didn't have the same cloud hanging over your head when it came to this place. You saw it through different eyes, and you helped me see it through different eyes too."

Her heart rate started to quicken. "But you have reasons for how you feel. I don't want you to hang onto something that you'll always associate with something bad from your childhood. You need to move on. You need to let go."

"Like you did?"

It was like a dozen little caterpillars crawling gently up her spine. "What do you mean?"

He reached for her hand. "You're the bravest woman I've ever met, Phoebe. And the one with the biggest heart. I'm sorry I left you in Rome. I'm sorry I left you to travel home alone."

She pulled her hand back. "I'm not." She couldn't help how blunt the words were.

"What do you mean?"

She turned away from him and looked at the array of desserts in front of her. She didn't want him touching her. She didn't want little electrical sparks shooting up her arms and heading straight to her heart. She picked up a slice of pie and a fork. She stabbed at the pie. "I mean, it was good for me. It was probably what I needed. Life is about looking after yourself. The first time I got on the plane it was for you—and for my mom. I could tell myself there was a reason to do it. I *needed* that money. I needed to complete the job. But the second time? It was for me. It was to tell myself I could do it. I didn't need anyone else. I could do this on my own—on my own terms. It was more important than you could ever imagine."

Matteo shifted uncomfortably in the seat next to her, eyeing the way her fork continued to stab at the pie.

"And what did you learn?"

She licked her lips. "I learned I could trust myself. I learned I could do anything." Her voice wavered a little. "I learned I could live this life on my own."

He reached over; the hand holding the fork was trembling and she hadn't even noticed. He put his warm hand over hers. "And do you want to? Because I believe, Phoebe, that you can do anything you want to do."

She swallowed and gulped, letting the plate rest down on her coat.

He kept talking. "You're beautiful and you're talented. I'm so lucky that I met you. Every day I regret leaving you behind. I was so focused on my sister and my family that I didn't realize my family reached further than my blood. I didn't realize my heart had already decided that you were family too."

Her hand froze. "What do you mean?"

He gave her a half-smile. "I mean, that this house, you, taught me to look ahead, to look to the future. The memories I have about this house are now about you, Phoebe. You even helped me remember some happy memories as a child here too. And you were right. Right about my sister and brother."

"How is your sister?"

"Brianna's good. She can't wait to meet you. Jay— and I might be biased—is possibly the most beautiful baby on the entire planet. And Brianna's well. Apart from being mad at me, and using a few choice words." He paused for a second. "But she understands. She understands why I didn't tell her. Not that she's happy." He shook his head and lowered it slightly. "She was particularly unhappy when she heard I'd left you in Rome when I got the news about her labor."

Phoebe pushed herself back in the chair. She was trying to take in what he was saying. But she'd been left in Rome feeling as if she'd misinterpreted everything. She couldn't feel like that again. She *wouldn't* feel like that again.

She glanced down at the pie on the plate on her lap. It had been well and truly desecrated.

Phoebe looked up into Matteo's eyes. They seemed sincere, but all she could think about right now was the ache in her heart.

"Why did you leave me in Rome, Matteo?"

He opened his mouth. The easiest thing for him to say was to repeat that it was all for Brianna.

"I was afraid."

She blinked. "You were afraid?"

He nodded. "I told myself I was protecting you—leaving you like that."

She gulped. "Well, it certainly didn't feel like that."

"I know. I thought I could never be enough for you. You're so open and honest, Phoebe. You're so full of life. You grab life. You want it. And you love with your whole heart."

She nodded and bit her lip. "And what about you, Matteo?" She understood more than he'd already said.

He shook his head. "I didn't think I could do that. I've never done it before. I've never been able to."

"Why?" She pushed him. She knew she had to.

He lifted his eyes to meet hers. "Because I don't want to open myself up. I don't want to open myself to the same kind of hurt I felt before."

Pain was written all over his face. Her fingers ached to reach out and touch him. But Matteo wasn't quite ready for that. She needed everything. She needed to know that he could love her just as much as she loved him.

"When your mother died? But you already have. Don't you see that? You opened yourself when you told me about your mother. You did it again when you told your brother and sister."

He nodded slowly. But her insides twisted. She

needed more. He was almost there. But he had to get there on his own. She couldn't do it for him.

She set the plate down on the table with a bang. "What do you want, Matteo? Why am I here?"

"You're here so I can say sorry." The words came out quickly—almost automatically.

She blinked. "Well, you've said it. I've heard it."

He tried to reach for her hands again but she brushed him off. "Please, Phoebe..."

"Please, Phoebe, what? What is this? What do you want me to say? I'm glad your sister is well, Matteo. I'm glad she has a healthy baby. I know you sold the house in Rome, great. And, as for why you don't want to sell this place?" The anger was starting to dissipate from her voice. She looked around the room. "That's entirely up to you. Maybe this place just needed a face lift." She shook her head, "Maybe you just needed to open the shutters." She couldn't help the metaphor.

Matteo shook his head. "What I needed, Phoebe, was you."

She stood up and walked over to the glass doors looking out over Mecox Bay. Matteo was right behind her and he gently laid his hand on her shoulder. "And maybe, what you needed was me."

She spun around to face him, tears brimming in her eyes. She pressed her hands up against her heart. "How can you say that? How can you? You were the first person I kissed since Jason died. The first person I actually *felt* something for. I didn't expect it. I wasn't looking for it. But it just happened. And I thought you were right there alongside me. But I was imagining it. I made a fool of myself. And now this? You ask me here?" Her voice was getting louder and louder. "Is this just to remind me about the time we spent here? Is this just to rub my face in it? Because you've still not told me why I'm here. You've still not told me what you want."

Matteo reached up and touched her cheek. "Because what I want is you, Phoebe. I want you to give me a chance. I'm sorry, for leaving you behind. I'm sorry for not being there on the flight with you. I want to make this work. Ever since I've met you, I've felt differently. You're like no one I've ever met before. You see the good in people. You walk into a room and just bring the light with you." He was smiling at her again. "I love being around you, Phoebe. I've always been a worka-holic and I'm not like that with you. When I'm around you, all I can think about is you." He pressed his hand against his heart. "I love you, Phoebe. I'll say it. I'll say it out loud for the world to hear. I don't care I've only known you for a couple of months. Every day for the last month, all I've thought about is you. Every day I've wanted to speak to you—to message you."

"Then why didn't you?"

He met her gaze with his bright green eyes. "Because I hadn't done what I should have. You challenged me before I left Rome. You told me I had to be honest with my sister and brother. I couldn't make excuses any-more for not telling them the truth. It didn't feel right, to come back and ask you to be part of my life when I hadn't taken the journey you'd challenged me to take. You'd faced your fears, Phoebe." His voice dropped. "I hadn't."

She sucked in a deep breath. "You thought I wouldn't want to be with you until you'd told your family?"

He closed his eyes for a second. "I thought I prob-ably didn't deserve you if I hadn't. I was still so wor-ried. I was watching Brianna the whole time. What if she had become ill? How fair would it be to ask you to be part of a family that could potentially be dealing with health problems for a long time?"

She tilted her head to one side. "And how fair would it be to ask you to be part of my life when my mother has just finished her cancer treatment? It could come back, then I'll spend all my time taking her for treatments and worrying about taking care of her. Do you see how ridiculous that sounds, Matteo? Family is family. What if you're ill? What if I'm ill? None of this should matter. The only thing that should matter is how two people feel about each other."

He nodded. "You're right. You're always right, Phoebe. It seems that even when I plan to tell a woman how much I love her I get that wrong too."

She was frozen to the spot. She wasn't sure how to respond. Her heart was swelling in her chest. Partly because of his response, and partly because she was still cautious.

Matteo stepped in front of her. "I did plan something else." He held out his hand toward her. "Will you come with me?"

As she lifted her hand toward his, he paused. "Wait a minute—do you want to slip off your coat?"

She glanced down. She was a little embarrassed to admit she was wearing the yellow dress underneath—the one he'd caught her dancing in. But she tilted her chin toward him as she undid the buttons on her bright green raincoat and handed it to him. Matteo left her coat over one of the leather chairs then held out his hand toward her again. There was a flicker in his eyes and the corners of his mouth turned upwards as his eyes took in her yellow dress.

He led her down the corridor to the atrium with the

curved staircase, pulling his phone from his pocket and pressing some buttons.

There was a gleam in his eyes. "I added a little extra to the house in the last few days."

She frowned and looked around. She couldn't see anything different. "What?"

Gentle music filled the air around them. The music from Phoebe's favorite musical. She couldn't help but smile.

"May I have this dance?" Matteo asked.

"Do you know what you're doing?" she asked.

He raised his eyebrows. "Around you? Apparently not. But I'm willing to spend a lifetime finding out."

She was holding her breath as she slid her hand into his. "I believe you need to start on the stairs," he said as he led her up the curved staircase, then stood a little underneath her.

It was silly. It was ridiculous. But it was exactly what she'd dreamed of. Matteo was just underneath her. He wasn't in a suit—just a simple pair of dress trousers and white shirt.

This time when he looked up at her there were no shadows in his eyes—only sincerity. His gaze was fixed entirely on her.

Her heart was playing a pitter-patter kind of tune in her chest. It had taken three years to kiss someone again. It had taken three years for her to find the courage to step onto a plane again—and whether he believed it or not, Matteo had given her the boost to do that. But was she really ready to give her heart away again?

The music was infectious. Her body started to sway in time to the tune, her feet soon following. Matteo was watching her the whole time. She moved up and down the staircase but as she reached the last few steps Matteo held out his arms to lift her down onto the main floor. One hand fitted snugly at her waist, the other held her hand tightly as he started to move around the room. Matteo could dance. He held her tightly to him as he swept her around the atrium. "How do you feel about doing this, every day, for the rest of your life?"

Her footsteps slowed. "How can I trust you, Matteo? What do you have to give me?"

He didn't hesitate. "My heart. It's yours. Forever. I hadn't realized that I needed to learn to trust. To open the shutters. To put myself out there. So, I'm here now. My heart. From this point on, we're family. You and me. For always."

Phoebe snaked her hands around his neck. "I might have some conditions."

He picked her up and swirled her around. "Name them."

She was smiling as her feet touched the ground again. "I might want you to dance me around every room in the house."

"Done."

"I might want the same amount of flowers in every room. I love them. The orange gerberas were particularly ingenious." She raised her eyebrows. "You might have a good eye."

"Done. Anything else?"

She stood on tiptoes and whispered in his ear. "We might need to reach a more formal agreement."

For a second, his brow furrowed. "How?"

This time it was her turn for there to be a twinkle in her eye. "It might involve a certain book, in my favorite room in the house."

Matteo gave her a wide smile as he slipped her hand

into his and led her down the corridor. "I'm not quite sure what you mean," he said as he winked at her. "I think you'll have to show me…"

# EPILOGUE

*New Year's Eve*

THERE WERE A million little butterflies currently beating their wings in her stomach. Phoebe's mother smoothed down her veil. "You look beautiful, darling. I've never felt so proud." Phoebe's heart swelled in her chest as she bent forward and kissed her mother on the cheek.

"Neither have I. Love you, Mom. I'm so glad we're doing this together."

There was a sweep of royal blue satin as Brianna appeared at the entrance of the door with three champagne glasses on a tray. "A toast," she declared. "To my new sister-in-law, and my son's honorary nanna." Phoebe's hands were shaking as she took a tiny sip.

"I'm too nervous. I can't drink."

Brianna and her mother laughed as her mother handed over her bouquet of yellow roses and green leaves. "Then, let's not keep the groom waiting."

Phoebe sucked in a deep breath and placed her hand on the smooth satin of her bodice. Brianna nodded and picked up her own bouquet. "Maid of honor first." She smiled as she disappeared out the door.

Phoebe's mother crooked her elbow. "Come on, then.

Let me make Matteo Bianchi the happiest man on the planet."

Phoebe slid her arm into her mother's and walked down the long corridor of the Hampton house. The whole house was buzzing with excitement; it was filled with their family and friends—just the way it should be. It seemed as if half of Italy were here to celebrate their wedding.

This was the way the house had always felt for Phoebe, as if it should be full of people, full of life, and finally Matteo had agreed.

She reached the top of the curved staircase and paused for a second. The whole wedding party was gathered in the huge hall, underneath the glass atrium. Outside the night sky was black, but just as she reached the top of the stairs fireworks started going off outside, sending streaks of pink, blue and red across the sky.

Matteo was waiting. His eyes only on her.

The dark suit with yellow tie to match her roses showed off his sallow skin and dark green eyes. His hair was flopping around his forehead—just the way she loved it—and, as she and her mother walked down the last few steps, his hand was waiting for hers.

"You look stunning," he whispered.

"You're not too bad yourself."

When he'd proposed a few months ago and asked her where she wanted to marry she didn't have a single doubt. It had to be here. It had to be in the family home. And it had to be on New Year's Eve, when they'd shared their first kiss.

The library was too small to fit all their guests, so the ceremony was taking place in the sitting room overlooking the gardens and Mecox Bay.

As they walked through to where the celebrant was

waiting, the glass doors were open to the garden and the white marquee outside fluttered in the wind.

Vittore stood proudly as his brother's best man, and Brianna served as her maid of honor as almost one-year-old Jay slept in his cradle in the corner of the room.

Phoebe turned to face Matteo. The celebrant looked at them as he checked his watch. "Are we ready to begin?"

More fireworks lit up the dark night sky outside as Phoebe slid her hands into Matteo's. And instead of sticking with tradition, they recited their vows together.

*"To have and to hold, from this day forward, for better for worse, for richer for poorer, in sickness and in health, to love and to cherish, till death do us part."*

And Mrs. Bianchi kissed her new husband as the ball dropped in Times Square and the world welcomed in the New Year.

* * * * *

*If you enjoyed this story, check out
these other great reads from Scarlet Wilson*

*THE MYSTERIOUS ITALIAN HOUSEGUEST
CHRISTMAS IN THE BOSS'S CASTLE
A BABY TO SAVE THEIR MARRIAGE
HIS LOST-AND-FOUND BRIDE*

*All available now!*

# MILLS & BOON®
## Hardback – January 2018

## ROMANCE

| | |
|---|---|
| **Alexei's Passionate Revenge** | Helen Bianchin |
| **Prince's Son of Scandal** | Dani Collins |
| **A Baby to Bind His Bride** | Caitlin Crews |
| **A Virgin for a Vow** | Melanie Milburne |
| **Martinez's Pregnant Wife** | Rachael Thomas |
| **His Merciless Marriage Bargain** | Jane Porter |
| **The Innocent's One-Night Surrender** | Kate Hewitt |
| **The Consequence She Cannot Deny** | Bella Frances |
| **The Italian Billionaire's New Year Bride** | Scarlet Wilson |
| **The Prince's Fake Fiancée** | Leah Ashton |
| **Tempted by Her Greek Tycoon** | Katrina Cudmore |
| **United by Their Royal Baby** | Therese Beharrie |
| **Pregnant with His Royal Twins** | Louisa Heaton |
| **The Surgeon King's Secret Baby** | Amy Ruttan |
| **Forbidden Night with the Duke** | Annie Claydon |
| **Tempted by Dr Off-Limits** | Charlotte Hawkes |
| **Reunited with Her Army Doc** | Dianne Drake |
| **Healing Her Boss's Heart** | Dianne Drake |
| **The Rancher's Baby** | Maisey Yates |
| **Taming the Texan** | Jules Bennett |

# MILLS & BOON®
## Large Print – January 2018

## ROMANCE

| | |
|---|---|
| **The Tycoon's Outrageous Proposal** | Miranda Lee |
| **Cipriani's Innocent Captive** | Cathy Williams |
| **Claiming His One-Night Baby** | Michelle Smart |
| **At the Ruthless Billionaire's Command** | Carole Mortimer |
| **Engaged for Her Enemy's Heir** | Kate Hewitt |
| **His Drakon Runaway Bride** | Tara Pammi |
| **The Throne He Must Take** | Chantelle Shaw |
| **A Proposal from the Crown Prince** | Jessica Gilmore |
| **Sarah and the Secret Sheikh** | Michelle Douglas |
| **Conveniently Engaged to the Boss** | Ellie Darkins |
| **Her New York Billionaire** | Andrea Bolter |

## HISTORICAL

| | |
|---|---|
| **The Major Meets His Match** | Annie Burrows |
| **Pursued for the Viscount's Vengeance** | Sarah Mallory |
| **A Convenient Bride for the Soldier** | Christine Merrill |
| **Redeeming the Rogue Knight** | Elisabeth Hobbes |
| **Secret Lessons with the Rake** | Julia Justiss |

## MEDICAL

| | |
|---|---|
| **The Surrogate's Unexpected Miracle** | Alison Roberts |
| **Convenient Marriage, Surprise Twins** | Amy Ruttan |
| **The Doctor's Secret Son** | Janice Lynn |
| **Reforming the Playboy** | Karin Baine |
| **Their Double Baby Gift** | Louisa Heaton |
| **Saving Baby Amy** | Annie Claydon |

# MILLS & BOON®
## Hardback – February 2018

## ROMANCE

| | |
|---|---|
| **The Secret Valtinos Baby** | Lynne Graham |
| **A Bride at His Bidding** | Michelle Smart |
| **The Greek's Ultimate Conquest** | Kim Lawrence |
| **Claiming His Nine-Month Consequence** | Jennie Lucas |
| **Bought with the Italian's Ring** | Tara Pammi |
| **A Proposal to Secure His Vengeance** | Kate Walker |
| **Redemption of a Ruthless Billionaire** | Lucy Ellis |
| **Shock Heir for the Crown Prince** | Kelly Hunter |
| **The Spanish Millionaire's Runaway Bride** | Susan Meier |
| **Stranded with Her Greek Tycoon** | Kandy Shepherd |
| **Reunited with Her Italian Billionaire** | Nina Singh |
| **Falling for His Convenient Queen** | Therese Beharrie |
| **The Doctor's Wife for Keeps** | Alison Roberts |
| **Twin Surprise for the Italian Doc** | Alison Roberts |
| **Falling for His Best Friend** | Emily Forbes |
| **Reunited with Her Parisian Surgeon** | Annie O'Neil |
| **From Bachelor to Daddy** | Meredith Webber |
| **A Surgeon to Heal Her Heart** | Janice Lynn |
| **For the Sake of His Heir** | Joanne Rock |
| **Rich Rancher's Redemption** | Maureen Child |

# MILLS & BOON®
## Large Print – February 2018

## ROMANCE

Claimed for the Leonelli Legacy — Lynne Graham
The Italian's Pregnant Prisoner — Maisey Yates
Buying His Bride of Convenience — Michelle Smart
The Tycoon's Marriage Deal — Melanie Milburne
Undone by the Billionaire Duke — Caitlin Crews
His Majesty's Temporary Bride — Annie West
Bound by the Millionaire's Ring — Dani Collins
Whisked Away by Her Sicilian Boss — Rebecca Winters
The Sheikh's Pregnant Bride — Jessica Gilmore
A Proposal from the Italian Count — Lucy Gordon
Claiming His Secret Royal Heir — Nina Milne

## HISTORICAL

Courting Danger with Mr Dyer — Georgie Lee
His Mistletoe Wager — Virginia Heath
An Innocent Maid for the Duke — Ann Lethbridge
The Viking Warrior's Bride — Harper St. George
Scandal and Miss Markham — Janice Preston

## MEDICAL

Tempted by the Bridesmaid — Annie O'Neil
Claiming His Pregnant Princess — Annie O'Neil
A Miracle for the Baby Doctor — Meredith Webber
Stolen Kisses with Her Boss — Susan Carlisle
Encounter with a Commanding Officer — Charlotte Hawkes
Rebel Doc on Her Doorstep — Lucy Ryder

# MILLS & BOON®

## Why shop at millsandboon.co.uk?

Each year, thousands of romance readers find their
perfect read at millsandboon.co.uk. That's because
we're passionate about bringing you the very best
romantic fiction. Here are some of the advantages
of shopping at www.millsandboon.co.uk:

* **Get new books first**—you'll be able to buy your
  favourite books one month before they hit
  the shops

* **Get exclusive discounts**—you'll also be able to buy
  our specially created monthly collections, with up
  to 50% off the RRP

* **Find your favourite authors**—latest news,
  interviews and new releases for all your favourite
  authors and series on our website, plus ideas for
  what to try next

* **Join in**—once you've bought your favourite books,
  don't forget to register with us to rate, review and
  join in the discussions

Visit **www.millsandboon.co.uk**
for all this and more today!